"It doesn't matter."

Angie reached for him, ~~curled her fingers~~ around his shoulder. He was her only anchor. She needed him. Her voice hoarse, she whispered, "It matters to me."

He looked at her squarely. "Five years. You left me five years ago."

She gasped. Not months, but years. Years of her life had vanished.

Instantly he covered her hand with his. Something in her stomach, warm and deep, fluttered. No matter what happened, she still responded to his most casual touch.

"Your daddy kindly answered a few questions for me. He said when you were done playing house with a man who wasn't your social equal, you begged him to bail you out. When your memory returns, I'll have a few questions for you."

"Like...?"

"For starters...why the hell are you sleeping in my bed?"

Dear Reader,

Silhouette is celebrating our 20th anniversary in 2000, and the latest powerful, passionate, provocative love stories from Silhouette Desire are as hot as that steamy summer weather!

For August's MAN OF THE MONTH, the fabulous BJ James begins her brand-new miniseries, MEN OF BELLE TERRE. In *The Return of Adams Cade*, a self-made millionaire returns home to find redemption in the arms of his first love.

Beloved author Cait London delivers another knockout in THE TALLCHIEFS miniseries with *Tallchief: The Homecoming,* also part of the highly sensual Desire promotion BODY & SOUL. And Desire is proud to present *Bride of Fortune* by Leanne Banks, the launch title of FORTUNE'S CHILDREN: THE GROOMS, another exciting spin-off of the bestselling Silhouette FORTUNE'S CHILDREN continuity miniseries.

BACHELOR BATTALION marches on with Maureen Child's *The Last Santini Virgin,* in which a military man's passion for a feisty virgin weakens his resolve not to marry. *In Name Only* is how a sexy rodeo cowboy agrees to temporarily wed a pregnant preacher's daughter in the second book of Peggy Moreland's miniseries TEXAS GROOMS. And Christy Lockhart reconciles a once-married couple who are stranded together in a wintry cabin during *One Snowbound Weekend....*

So indulge yourself by purchasing all six of these summer delights from Silhouette Desire...and read them in air-conditioned comfort.

Enjoy!

Joan Marlow Golan

Joan Marlow Golan
Senior Editor, Silhouette Desire

Please address questions and book requests to:
Silhouette Reader Service
U.S.: 3010 Walden Ave., P.O. Box 1325, Buffalo, NY 14269
Canadian: P.O. Box 609, Fort Erie, Ont. L2A 5X3

One Snowbound Weekend...

CHRISTY LOCKHART

Published by Silhouette Books
America's Publisher of Contemporary Romance

For Pam, brainstorming partner who believes;
for Whitney, chief researcher,
and for Lisa, my Designated Worrier.

Also for Dad, 'tis great to have you in my life…

 SILHOUETTE BOOKS

ISBN 0-373-76314-X

ONE SNOWBOUND WEEKEND…

Copyright © 2000 by Christine Pacheco

Visit Silhouette at www.eHarlequin.com

Printed in U.S.A.

Books by Christy Lockhart

Silhouette Desire

Hart's Baby #1193
Let's Have a Baby! #1212
The Cowboy's Christmas Baby #1260
One Snowbound Weekend... #1314

Previously published as Christine Pacheco

Silhouette Desire

The Rogue and the Rich Girl #960
Lovers Only #1054
A Husband in Her Stocking #1113

CHRISTY LOCKHART

married her real-life hero, Jared, who proved to her that dreams really do come true. They live in Colorado with their two children, Raymond and Whitney.

Christy remembers always wanting to be a writer. She even talked her elementary school librarian into "publishing" her books. She notes always preferring romances because they're about that special moment when dreams are possible and the future is a gift to unfold.

You can write to Christy at P.O. Box 448, Eastlake, CO 80614.

One

Shane Masters's ax froze in midswing.

Blinded by the wind-whipped snow, his eyes had to be playing tricks on him.

There was no way his ex-wife was fighting her way through a Colorado blizzard toward him.

Hardhat, Shane's yellow Labrador, barked and ran circles around Shane's legs, warning him about the approaching stranger. That meant Shane wasn't hallucinating.

He dropped his ax on top of the woodpile and stared into the distance. Steps unsteady and her slender body beaten by ice daggers driven from the sky, she continued onward.

If he didn't resent Angie's intrusion into the life he'd rebuilt, he might have admired her courage.

As it was, he'd sworn he never wanted to see her

again. Over five years ago, he'd toasted that determination with a whiskey bottle and never looked back.

Narrowing his green eyes and folding his arms across his chest, he waited.

When she was about five feet away, she pitched herself at him.

Instinctively he caught her, unprepared for the feel of her trembling, feminine body pressing against him and the strong, unwelcome wave of desire that walloped him.

"Thank God I made it home," she whispered.

Home? Columbine Crossing hadn't really ever been her home, and she hadn't been back since their divorce.

"The thought of you, waiting for me, worrying about me, kept me going when I wasn't sure I could take another step."

Her words plowed reality back into focus.

She burrowed her head against his down-covered shoulder, and tendrils of her light brown hair cascaded down his coat. Then she laid one hand on his chest, near where his heart suddenly thundered.

His blood, dulled by the wind's wicked bite, slowly warmed. And his insides tightened painfully in physical response to her innocent touch.

He didn't welcome the reaction, nor did he want to be vulnerable to the woman who'd destroyed his trust and shattered his heart.

Hardhat barked, and Shane forced himself to go rigid. Although his gut twisted, urging him to draw her closer, he released the hand he'd unthinkingly slid around her slender waist.

Angie uncurled her fingers and glanced up at him, a question in her wide, expressive blue eyes.

It was then, when he really looked at her, that he saw the angry cut carved on her forehead, vivid red splashed against the paleness of her skin. He didn't want to care. But anger couldn't replace concern. "What happened to your head?"

She reached a trembling hand to the cut. Wincing, she said, "I don't know..." Her brow furrowed as she frowned. "I must have hit it on the steering wheel of the car."

"What car?"

"Our car. The one we bought in Durango." The words were slowly formed, as if concentrating took huge effort. "Maybe you were right about it needing a new alternator."

His mind raced to keep up with what she was saying.

"When I woke up, I was...was in the ditch."

He scowled, searching her features. Her blue eyes glazed over. And it hit him.

She was in shock.

All the words he'd dreamed of hurling at her dried in his mouth. "You were in an accident?"

"I guess so." She swayed.

He grabbed her again, this time swinging her from the ground and up into his arms.

"I'm okay," she protested.

"Right." With strides shortened by the foot of fresh snow, he started toward his cabin.

"I knew you'd take care of me."

He ground his back teeth together. Until this moment, he couldn't have said he'd have taken care of her. In fact, that was the last thing he wanted to do.

Reaching up an icy hand, she traced the line of his cheek, just the way she had the night they first discovered each other, when he'd taught her about passion....

But she'd given up the right to touch him—physically

or emotionally—when she'd divorced him to marry another man.

Running ahead of them, Hardhat pushed through the snow with his nose, flinging flakes everywhere.

"When did we get a dog?"

"When did we get a dog?" he echoed.

"I don't remember..."

Something more icy than the snow shivered down his spine.

"What's her name?"

"His name is Hardhat."

"Why don't I know that...?"

Shane opened the cabin door. This much, she'd surely remember. He'd rented the small house the day before their wedding so she and his sister, Sarah, would have someplace other than a rickety trailer to call home.

He'd bought the cabin after Angie left, not out of any sense of nostalgia, but as a solid, constant reminder that women shattered hearts and devastated homes.

Inside, he kicked the door closed, locking out the storm's vicious lash.

Ignoring the fact he trampled snow across the honey-colored hardwood floor, he carried her into the living room and set her on the couch. "We need to get you out of those wet clothes," he said, yanking off his gloves and tossing them on the throw rug.

Hardhat immediately grabbed one and ran toward his mat, placing a triumphant paw on the glove.

"Angie? You need to take off your jacket."

"Where's Sarah?"

His brows drew together. His sister was at college, where she had been for two years. "With friends," he said.

Angie didn't respond, nor did she move.

Her hands, whitened from exposure to the brutal elements, trembled as she reached for the coat's zipper. How long had she been outside, and how far had she walked?

Shane didn't want the answers to matter. But they did.

She shivered uncontrollably, and her light brown hair fell forward, shielding her face and thankfully blocking the gratitude and adoration emanating from her sky-blue eyes.

Moving her hand aside, he took hold of the zipper's tab and parted the metal teeth.

A pendant glittered in the firelight.

He swallowed, hard.

Unable to help himself, he reached for the gold-dipped aspen leaf, tracing his fingertip across the raised veins in the metal, remembering…

As if it were yesterday, he recalled giving her the piece of jewelry. It had been their fourth date. He'd been young, poor, idealistic. She'd been young, rich and— he'd thought—different from other women.

She'd admired the aspen leaf, saying she'd never seen anything like it back east. He'd bought it for her.

Back then, purchasing the small trinket had been the financial equivalent of giving her the moon. Buying it had wiped out his last dollar.

She had protested his extravagance, saying he should spend his hard-earned money on Sarah and his new business. Softly Angie had added that being with him was all she needed.

Shane's hardened heart had started to crack in that moment.

When he'd insisted she accept the gift, she'd lifted her hair, and he'd gently fastened the clasp at her nape.

And she still had the reminder of their time together. Amazing.

"Is something wrong?"

"Wrong?" he asked, voice raw, as if it had been dragged through rusty nails.

"You're scowling."

"Nothing," he said, pulling his hand back and shoving aside the past.

With a physical gentleness he didn't feel emotionally, he shucked the jacket from her shoulders and dropped it beside his single glove. She looked at him through the fringe of her hair, and he noticed that her lower lip quivered. She was getting to him....

Her teeth chattered, the sound amplified in the quiet. He'd been so wrapped up in his memories that he was neglecting to care for her properly.

Softly cursing, he moved into action, tossing a couple of logs on the dwindling fire, stoking the embers and fanning the flame.

Returning to her, he dropped to his knees, ignoring the winking aspen leaf nestled near her breast.

She curled her small hand around his shoulder the same way she might have once upon a time. Trying to ignore the touch, he drew off her shoes, pricey leather flats that had no place in a Rocky Mountain blizzard.

Her socks were soaked, and he pulled them off, exposing the pale pink polish brushed across her toenails. *She'd never painted her toenails before.*

He shoved aside the thoughts and the anger that still nipped at his soul.

She no longer mattered to him.

Her denim jeans were frozen and stiff near the ankle, and he knew they needed to be removed, too. Damned if he'd do it, though.

He grabbed a throw from the back of the couch and settled it around her shoulders.

"Thank you," she murmured, tipping back her head and looking at him. Her hair fell away from her forehead, again exposing her wound.

In the dim light spilling through the large window, the cut seemed to ravage her skin.

He gritted his teeth. He'd already told himself she didn't matter.

But her vulnerability sliced through his carefully constructed defenses.

Against his will, he moved his finger across her skin, not touching the injury but feeling the sizzle of heat against frost.

She flinched, but didn't pull away.

"I need to call Doc Johnson."

"Dr. Johnson?" She pressed her fingers against her temples, as if hoping to soothe away the pain. "What about Dr. Kirk?"

"He retired." Was it possible that she'd truly forgotten the past few years? Surely it was the shock, nothing more....

Flames hissed and crackled, and his heart rate accelerated.

Pushing to his feet he said, "I'll be right back," before crossing to the master bedroom. He needed a lifeline to sanity, and she needed dry clothes.

Unable to reach Dr. Johnson at his office, Shane dialed the man's home phone number and succinctly detailed the situation, including the fact that Angie was conscious and coherent and seemed fine, as long as you didn't count the fact she was freezing cold and seemed to have no recollection of their divorce.

"That's entirely possible, young man," Dr. Johnson

said. "With the car accident, potential trauma to the brain...your Angie could be suffering from posttraumatic amnesia."

Amnesia. Breath rushed from Shane's lungs. "She needs to see you immediately."

"I completely agree, Shane, but you'd be risking further injury by trying to get her through the blizzard. I don't have all the equipment to run a complete neurological examination. She needs to go to a hospital, but it's doubtful we could get her there safely."

"So what the hell am I supposed to do with her?"

"Keep her calm, give her aspirin for the pain. Watch her for the possibility of a concussion. As soon as the roads are plowed, we can send an ambulance or you can bring her in. Of course, if you have an emergency, call right away."

"That's it?"

"Sorry, Shane."

"What do I do about her amnesia?"

"Unfortunately, there's nothing you can do, except try and keep her quiet," the doctor said.

"What about her memory? When will she get it back?"

"That's anyone's guess, young man. Could be twenty minutes, could be next week."

"And it might not happen at all," Shane said flatly.

"I can't say. But the last thing you need is for Angie to panic. She's been through quite enough trauma as it is. Don't you agree?"

Shane's grip tightened on the phone. "I should let her believe she's my wife?"

"If that keeps her from panicking and potentially causing more damage, yes."

Shane didn't like it. Before he could question the doctor further, static chewed up the phone line, and the connection died.

He was stuck, his ex-wife thinking they were still starry-eyed in love. And he couldn't tell her any different.

He dropped the phone's handset back into its cradle. Shell-shocked, he returned to the living room.

"Shane? What did the doctor say?"

"Take two aspirin and call him in the morning."

Her attempted smile faded before it formed. A part of him, one he thought no longer existed, stirred.

He crossed to her and placed his hands on her shoulders. She fit his cupped palms perfectly, as if they had always been two parts of the same whole.

To distract himself from the unwelcome, impossible thought, he said, "You still need to change out of those wet clothes. As soon as you've done that, I'll clean and bandage the wound on your forehead."

Snowflakes had melted into her hair, the dampness making the color appear a couple of shades darker than he remembered. And now there was an alluring hint of copper buried between the strands. He struggled to resist the urge to bury his fingers in its thickness and hold her close.

But it was her eyes that really got to him. They were wide, and focused unblinkingly on him.

In the five years since he'd seen her, he'd forgotten how very powerful her eyes were. The color, a blue as vibrant as a sun-drenched sky, was potent, making him think of lovemaking and forever in a single blink. But he didn't dare forget they were a great shield for deceit.

"Did we have a fight?" she asked softly.

He released her. "A fight?"

"Is that why you're angry with me?"

"I'm not angry," he denied, the doctor's warning to keep her calm echoing in Shane's mind.

"You always scowl like that when you're upset."

He dragged his fingers through his dark hair.

"You do that, too."

In frustration, he exhaled. Damn it. How was it possible for her to remember so much and forget even more?

As she had done earlier, she stroked the side of his unshaven cheekbone. The gentle abrasion shuddered through him.

"What did I do to upset you?" She paused at the cleft in his chin, as intimately as she had five years ago.

"Shane?"

She still said his name the same way, with a husk of sensuality that skipped across his skin like the slide of silk.

"Did I do something terrible?"

"No," he lied, cuffing her wrist and moving her hand away.

"Then why don't you want me touching you?"

"I need to clean that cut."

"You're avoiding my question."

Unconsciously he took hold of her again. He didn't want to care for her, protect her. He'd sworn he never wanted to set eyes on her again. Yet she was injured and alone, dependent on him.

Like it or not, he had an obligation. And Shane took his obligations seriously, had since he was nine years old and his mother deserted the family for a rich man and an easier life. His father had worked two jobs and drowned his sorrows when he was home, leaving Shane to care for his younger sister after school and on week-ends. When he was nineteen and his dad died, Shane had naturally taken over raising Sarah.

And now he'd do what was expected of him, even if living Angie's lie sat on his shoulders like a load of concrete. "You're hurt," he said. Then, softly, he added, "And you need to rest. Since we can't get to town, I get to play doctor."

"I'd like that."

Tension fragmented the atmosphere.

Her gaze searched his face, looking, he figured, for anything less than honesty.

"Shane…"

"We'll talk about it later."

"All of it? Why you're angry, what I did, why you don't want me touching you?"

Keep her calm. "Yeah."

Her eyes darkened with distrust. His promise had been insincere and she'd heard the cop-out in his tone. But hell, short of taking her in his arms and finishing what she was so innocently trying to start, Shane knew there was nothing he could do.

Now, if only he weren't so damn tempted…

Two

Even though the heartbeat of sensual awareness pulsed between them, she realized Shane was telling her what she wanted to hear, nothing more. Angie studied the pine-green depths of his eyes and saw the shadow of deceit. "Why are you lying to me?"

He dragged a hand through his hair, scattering a lock of dark brown across his forehead. "Can we postpone this until you're feeling better?"

Angie prided herself on her strength. Without it, she would never have walked away from her father and the marriage he'd been arranging for her.

She'd shown courage in defying expectations, and she wouldn't stop asking questions now.

"I'll get the first aid kit," Shane said, severing the contact of their gazes. He pushed to his feet and headed into the bathroom.

Restless and confused, she tossed the colorful Navajo

blanket back from her shoulders and moved to the fire-place, crouching to ruffle the dog's fur. Hardhat was adorable, especially with the red bandanna tied around his neck. It was odd that she couldn't remember their dog. It was even stranger that she couldn't remember her fight with Shane, no matter how hard she tried.

But their lovemaking...*that* she remembered....

He returned, freezing when she saw her petting the dog. "The doctor said you need rest."

"How did we end up getting a dog?"

"Hardhat was a stray on a construction site in town. One day he followed me home and never left."

"When?"

Carefully, his expression neutral, he said, "Recently."

"Stop with the half truths, Shane."

His knuckles whitened against the bottle of peroxide.

"How recently?" she repeated.

"Angie—"

"You told me we'd talk about it," she reminded him.

"Later. I said we'd talk about it later."

She stood and squared her shoulders, facing him. "We made an agreement to always be open and honest with each other. Do you remember?"

He put the first aid kit and the peroxide on the coffee table. "I'm not keeping secrets."

"Then help me understand." She loved Shane with her whole heart and soul. If something was wrong, she'd do anything, *anything* to fix it.

Ignoring the thudding ache in her temples she asked, "Why don't you want me to touch you? You usually encourage me to feel your body, massage the knots out after you've worked all day, wash your back when you shower and then dry you before you carry me to bed...."

"Do you remember the day we moved in here? You were determined we'd have some kind of honeymoon. Sarah stayed with Kurt Majors's family and you insisted we make love in nearly every room of our new home in the first twenty-four hours. We tried the kitchen first."

His nostrils flared, and a corresponding awareness cascaded through her insides. "What happened between us?" she asked quietly.

"Dammit, Angie, the doctor said—"

"Forget the doctor, Shane." She took a step toward him. His breathing changed, and she took a second step. "This is about you and me. About us." Stopping only inches from him, she placed her hand on his chest, feeling his strength beneath the soft cotton of his flannel shirt. "I want answers."

"I don't think you're up to it."

He placed his hand on top of hers, holding her still and not letting her hand wander. That wasn't like him. Nor was the tension sketched beside his eyes.

"Let me decide that, okay? I need to understand why the man I married is acting like a stranger. I need to know why you're shutting me out."

Indecision clouded across the green of his eyes, making them murky. Eventually he sighed. "You asked if we had a fight. We did."

"We've had other fights."

"Not like this."

"Worse?"

"Yeah."

Wind slashed against the large windows, shaking them in their wooden casings.

Why couldn't she remember? Something so important should fill her mind, shouldn't it?

"Leave it at that, Angie."

"But—"

"You're here, you're safe. There's time for the rest later."

"Was it bad enough to ruin our relationship?"

"Angie—"

"Was it?" she repeated breathlessly, demandingly.

"Yeah."

She swallowed the information, but didn't know what to do with it. Nothing made sense, and the harder she tried to remember, the more fuzzy her brain became.

She squeezed her eyes shut against the roar in her head and the ache in her heart.

"I need to clean that cut on your forehead."

"Shane—"

"Don't be so stubborn, Angie. Give in."

She didn't want to, but she knew he was right. "Okay," she said, nodding. "For now."

He released his hold on her, and her hand fell to her side, her palm still warm.

"Sit on the couch."

When she did, he crouched in front of her and poured peroxide on a cotton ball.

His touch tender, he feathered her hair back from her forehead and said, "This may sting."

"No more than this awkwardness between us."

"You never give up, do you?"

"You made me promise that I'd never give up on us. And I won't."

Their gazes locked, and the spikes of pain in his eyes stole her breath. She'd seen that kind of hurt there before, when he'd told her about his mother and the way she deserted him on his ninth birthday.

The ache in his eyes had intensified when he'd confided that he'd proposed to Delilah Clark, a girl he'd gone to high school with. Delilah said she'd marry him as long as he got rid of his sister.

Angie had held him that night, promising him she'd never walk out on him, no matter what.

Now, just like then, she wanted to cradle him. But this time, she knew he wouldn't appreciate it. Instead, she hugged her arms around her middle so she wouldn't do anything she'd regret.

He applied ointment and a bandage, his fingertips barely glancing off her skin.

"Thank you," she said.

"You need to take off those wet clothes." He stood and capped the brown bottle, sliding it on the coffee table. "I'll get you a couple of aspirin first."

He offered his hand and she hesitated. He might not want her touch, but she craved his.

Patiently he waited, his mouth a tight line, revealing nothing. In fact, if she hadn't seen the thready pulse in his temple, she might have thought he felt nothing.

Finally, desperate for the connection, any connection, she slipped her hand against his palm. Maybe if she broke past the barrier of ice...

For a moment, his fingers closed around hers. Warmth and longing flooded her as he slowly pulled her up.

She swayed toward him. Her hopes of him softening died in that instant. He simply steadied her, then released her before turning on his booted heel. His steps away from her seemed to echo her loneliness off the hardwood floor.

Tears from Shane's rejection stinging her eyes, she crossed to their bedroom only to gasp aloud at the sight of it.

"Angie!" he called. "Are you okay?"

She heard his boots thundering on the flooring, but

she couldn't answer. Instead, she frantically grabbed hold of the doorjamb.

There were no traces of her anywhere in this room.

Their mismatched set of furniture—bought at a yard sale—was gone, replaced by a set of solid oak pieces. A bedspread, colorful with a southwestern design splashed on the fabric, lay across the mattress. But where was her pastel-colored quilt with the wedding-ring pattern?

"Angie?" he asked again, placing a hand on her shoulder.

"Where are my things?" Pulling away, she moved into the room, dropping to her knees and yanking open the bottom right-hand drawer where she usually kept her lingerie. She found his socks and briefs.

She slammed the drawer and reached for another, where she should find belts and hair accessories. Nothing. Frantically, she yanked open a third drawer and started shoving aside his sweaters hoping to find something—anything—of hers.

"Stop." Kneeling next to her, he clamped his hand around her wrist.

She looked up at the man she'd sworn she'd love forever, the man she'd given herself to, body and heart.

And she didn't recognize him.

"Answer me, Shane. Where are my things? Why is there no trace of me in this room? Was our fight so bad that you'd kick me out of your life like this?"

"You've got clothes in the closet."

Her breath rushed out. "In the closet?"

"On the shelves."

She didn't remember....

He slowly released his grip, but he didn't move away.

"But that's not all," she said softly, momentarily

squeezing her eyes shut. "You've changed, Shane. You're not the man I married."

"I'm the same as I've always been."

He still had the same good looks, the same scar beneath his chin from the childhood bike accident, the same angular jaw, the same intensely green eyes, the same thick, dark hair begging to be mussed, the same cleft in his chin where she'd rested her finger earlier.

He was still the same, yet so much...more. "You're harder." Broader, stronger, more rigid. *More man.* "Less loving. I remember the way you'd smile when you saw me, the way you'd reach for me, the way you'd carry me in here." Her voice broke as she finished, "The way you'd make love to me..."

He cursed softly. His eyes lightened a shade. If she didn't know otherwise, she might have thought she'd glimpsed tenderness.

But then it was gone, and night returned to the pine-forest depths of his eyes. Swimming in a sea of confusion, she got to her feet.

"When did we get this furniture?" she asked.

"I ordered it from the Mountain Majesty catalog you like."

Drawing her brows together, she whispered, "When?"

"Does it matter?"

"It does to me." She reached her hand to her forehead, and suddenly it became shockingly, frighteningly clear. "The accident. Our fight... I've forgotten, haven't I? I've blocked it out." Her heart raced. "I've lost part of my memory."

"There's time for all this later." He stood but thankfully didn't move toward her. "When you're feeling better, when you've rested."

"That's what you talked to Dr. Johnson about, isn't it? My memory loss."

"Angie—" he warned.

Suddenly she was more afraid than she ever remembered being. "How much, Shane? How much time have I lost?"

"I don't know." He spoke slowly, soothingly, his reassuring cadence the only lifeline she had to hold on to. "The doctor said it could be posttraumatic amnesia."

Her knees weakened. "What does that mean?" She sank onto the bed she didn't remember sharing with him.

"He won't know, exactly, unless he runs a complete neurological examination."

Twisting her hands together, she softly said, "And because of the weather, you can't get me to the hospital."

He nodded.

"So you're stuck with me."

"We're stuck with each other."

Oh, how she'd wanted him to deny it, to tell her that being with her wasn't a hardship.

"Your memory could come back all on its own."

She twisted her hands together. "When?"

"Anytime."

"What happens if it doesn't? What if it never comes back at all?"

"Don't," he warned, the word a soft growl. Devouring the distance in a couple of quick strides, he took hold of her upper arms, but there was nothing intimate about his grip.

"We don't have any information, so we can't hazard a guess. Dr. Johnson wouldn't."

She struggled to take it all in, but she was shivering, as if the cold was devouring her from the inside out.

"The best thing you can do is follow the doctor's orders. Rest, and change out of the wet clothes so you don't end up with a cold, as well."

"But—"

His grip tightened. "Do us both a favor. Quit arguing."

He released her, and the temperature plummeted. The howling wind and driving snow only made it worse.

Shane crossed to the closet and returned with a pair of sweatpants and matching shirt. At least these were familiar.

She grabbed for the hem of her damp sweater, only to wince when her muscles protested.

A pulse ticking in his temple, he offered his help.

"Thanks," she said.

He eased the sweater over her head, dropping it onto the floor and scooping up the sweatshirt. As he helped her into the soft fleece, his fingers skimmed her bare skin, raising awareness deep inside her.

She glanced at him, and he refused to meet her gaze. He wasn't looking at *her*.

Tears stung again, and she tried to blink them back.

"What about your jeans?"

"I can manage." Better that than having a man touch her who no longer wanted to...

When she stood and fumbled with the zipper's small tab, he said, "I'll do it."

His motions were deft and sure, not that that was a surprise. He'd undressed her dozens of times.

Yet there was something different knowing he was angry, recognizing he didn't want to be near her, realizing their marriage was no longer the happily-ever-after fairy tale she believed it to be.

He shimmied the damp, stiff denim past her hips and

down her thighs. Kneeling, he held the jeans while she stepped out of them.

Breath froze in her lungs.

His gaze swept upward as he looked at her, pausing midway up her body.

He sucked in a shallow breath, his eyes narrowing. Her body quickened in response to his unspoken need.

He touched her, gently.

Then, swearing softly, he dropped his hand, pushed to his feet and grabbed the aspirin he'd carried into the room.

Uncapping the bottle, he shook out two tablets and placed them on the bedside table, alongside a glass of water. "Call me if you need anything." The door closed behind him with a sharp click.

She needed so much from him—needed to be held, caressed, loved...the very things he wasn't offering.

Her head thundered. She wanted things back the way they had been before... Before... Before the fight she couldn't remember.

She'd demanded answers, and Shane had given a few. Maybe he'd been right in guessing she was better off not knowing. His honesty hadn't solved anything, it had only made it worse.

Finally, the pain ricocheting inside her head won. Angie gave in. Telling herself that maybe her memory would return if she rested, she pulled back the bedspread and crawled beneath the blanket.

She lay down and inhaled Shane's scent, that of mountain air and citrus spice. Another small thing that was familiar in a world tipped upside down. She found comfort in it.

She gave a soft sigh of relief. He might be angry, but he hadn't shut her out completely. When he'd taken off her jeans, sensuality had arced between them. That gave her a glimmer of hope.

She'd always been a fighter, and more than once Shane had said he admired that about her. Well, he'd never seen her fight like this before. She wanted Shane's love back, and she'd do anything to get it.

The only problem was, she didn't know where to start because the enemy was inside her own head....

She wasn't the only one with memory problems.

Shane shoved the bottle of aspirin back on the shelf in the kitchen and slammed the cupboard door.

Pivoting, he strode into the living room, Hardhat on his heels.

What the hell was Shane thinking, allowing his gaze to caress her the way his hands once had, forgetting the way she'd callously turned and run from their vows and commitment?

Oh, it was easy to forget, when all he could do was remember the way they'd talk and laugh, the way he shared his darkest secrets with her, her responses, soft and sensual, daring and demanding...her scent, perfume and shampoo mingling with feminine temptation...the feel of her yielding to his desires....

Having her pressed against him transported him back five years to a time he'd believed in love, and more, had actually taken a leap and trusted her with his heart.

Of all people, he should have realized that integrity didn't exist in the female species. His mother had proved that, and so had Delilah.

He'd decided never to get involved with a woman again. That resolve had lasted until he'd seen Angie at her aunt Emma's coffee shop. Angie had served him more than a drink—she'd served him sunshine and warmth, all with a bright smile. And the concrete encasing his heart had started to chip away.

He'd thought she was different, and when she'd married him, he'd *known* she was different.

Two months later, he'd learned his lesson. No woman, not even Angie, had integrity.

Grabbing his coat, he shrugged into it. He'd left the pile of wood outside, and if instinct proved right, it would only be a matter of time before the storm prevented him from going outside at all.

He opened the door and icy wind lashed at him, viciously chewing on his earlobes.

Suited his mood fine.

Hardhat tucked his tail between his legs and slunk back to the hearth. The dog might be a traitor, but he wasn't dumb.

Needing an outlet for the emotional energy churning in his gut, Shane battled his way to the woodpile, grabbed an armload of split pine and hauled it through the snow.

He opened his eyes wide in the driving wind, trying to vanquish the image of light brown hair and haunted blue eyes. It didn't help. He couldn't get rid of her, no matter how hard he tried.

Her arrival on his doorstep—a place not easy to find— brought dozens of questions to mind, mainly, why was she here? Was his home her destination? And if it was, why?

The Dear John letter she'd left behind stated she didn't want him to seek her out, said she never wanted to see him again, swore she'd never loved him. Their marriage had been a mistake, their love a lie.

His gut twisted as he remembered the pain, the disbelief, the grief that paralyzed.

He still hadn't wanted to believe it, so he'd traveled to Chicago to seek her out. There, her father had set him straight, saying that Angie had grown up, realized she'd made a mistake in marrying a poor boy and begged her father to come and get her, bailing her out of her mistake.

Shoving aside the intrusive thoughts, Shane struggled back through the front door. He was determined to find out what the hell she wanted with him, what havoc she intended to wreak, and get her back out of his life.

After stacking the first load of wood in the storage closet, he went back for a second, then third, ignoring the soft sounds drifting from the master bathroom.

She was supposed to be asleep. Then again, she'd never been great at following orders, especially his.

By the fourth trip, he'd exhausted himself battling the elements. With the door bolted against the raging fury, her soft sounds became more difficult to ignore.

Water ran. Obviously she was drinking from the same glass he'd used earlier this morning, an intimacy a wife would automatically take.

He swallowed.

She thought they were still married.

He dropped his outer clothes near the door and strode to the fireplace, grabbing the poker and stabbing the embers. Hardhat barked a protest as metal slammed against concrete.

Squatting, Shane reached for a log and tossed it on the grate. It promised to be a long day, even longer evening with his ex-wife tucked between *his* sheets.

Three

She was the same woman, yet totally different.

Toward evening, he stood in the doorway, his shoulder propped against the jamb, watching the gentle rise and fall of her chest as she slept...on his side of the bed.

Firelight from the living room flickered on her light brown hair. The strands sifted across the pillow, inviting his touch. "Angie?"

She didn't respond.

He entered the room, his bare feet silent on the oak floor.

The comforter snuggled her body, tucked around her shoulders, and only her face peeked from beneath the warmth of down. Shane reached to shake her awake, but stopped, captivated by the light playing on her face.

The cut looked obscene against the paleness of her skin, and he'd do anything to take that ache away from her. No one deserved to be hurt like that.

Without thinking, he succumbed to temptation, feathering his fingers into her hair, letting the rumpled strands wind around his knuckles like he used to.

Before he could pull his hand back, her eyes flickered open. A slow smile slipped across her lips, and they parted in silent greeting. "Shane..." Reaching up, she stroked his hand, as if they were lovers. "Are you coming to bed?"

Instinct warned of danger. "No." He loosened his grip on the silky lock of hair. No matter how tempting she was, no matter how he suddenly wanted to forget her desertion, he wouldn't get tangled in her web. He'd done that once and it had cost him his heart. "I made you some soup."

"Soup?"

"Chicken noodle. Figured it's always good when you're not feeling well."

She blinked, as if remembering the last few hours. The welcome in her eyes and on her mouth faded. "Oh. I'd forgotten." Her hand dropped away from his.

He shouldn't want her touch, not when he intended to get her back out of his life. "I'll bring it to you." He returned to the kitchen, hoping he'd find sanity there.

Slamming drawers and cupboards, he ladled the warmed soup into a bowl, then piled everything on a tray, grabbing a box of Saltine crackers from the counter on the way back to his room.

She wiggled into a sitting position, the comforter peeling back to reveal that she was wearing one of his T-shirts. Old and faded, the white cotton conformed to her, and her breasts pushed against the fabric.

While he'd brought in the firewood, she'd been doing more than drinking a glass of water. *She'd been undressing.*

An image of their past flashed in his mind. When she'd slept in anything at all, it had been one of his T-shirts and nothing else.

And she would still think it was okay.

That meant that beneath the covers, her long, shapely legs were bare. It felt like a hammer to the gut when he remembered the feel of those legs, wrapped around his naked waist as they sweetly made love.

"I hope you don't mind me changing," she said, as if reading his mind. "I was too hot in sweats."

"Sure," he lied. Forcing himself to refocus, he slid the tray onto the nightstand and saw her discarded clothes on the floor, the silk and lace of her bra on top of the pile.

His mouth dried.

"Thank you," she said softly, the words huskily drawn across a sleep-rubbed voice. "You're too good to me."

Shane offered her a cup of tea, two sugars stirred in, the way she always drank it.

She wrapped her hands around the mug, sipped from it, then wrinkled her nose. "I drink it black." She blinked. "Don't I?"

"You tell me." He folded his arms across his chest and waited.

Angie frowned, her brows pinched as if in pain. Her hand shook as she slid the tea back onto the tray.

She wrapped her hands across her shoulders again, in the same protective way she had earlier. She hadn't done that when he'd known her before. Just how much, he wondered, *didn't* he know about her?

He'd thought he knew every part of her, how she cried out his name when she teetered on the brink of fulfill-ment, the way she wiggled next to him, stealing the

sheets and seeking his heat after they made love, the
way her eyes darkened, like a storm on an alpine lake,
when she shyly initiated intimacy.

But he hadn't known a thing about her, not really. He
hadn't suspected she could run away from him, leaving
behind her clothes, a scrawled letter and a diamond ring
that winked damningly in the dull autumn light. He
hadn't known that her courage and declarations of love
had all been a lie.

"Your soup's getting cold." He turned to leave.

"Shane."

He paused, but he didn't look back.

"I can't fix our problem if you won't tell me what's
wrong." Her voice was a low, husky plead.

He told himself it had no effect on him. "It can't be
fixed, Angie."

Her head roared and blood thundered against her temples, echoing Shane's words. *It can't be fixed.*

She pressed the aspen leaf against her breast, holding
on to the feelings she'd had that day when she'd scooped
the hair from her neck and he fastened the clasp at her
nape.

Closing her eyes, she tried to fill in the blanks, only
to come up empty. She remembered meeting him at
Aunt Emma's coffee shop, the way his eyes had narrowed speculatively with distrust when she smiled at
him. That hadn't stopped her, though. She'd smiled even
brighter.

He'd returned the next day and asked what her name
was. By the third day, he confessed he'd never drunk
coffee before that week. On Thursday, their hands had
accidentally touched; on Friday, he'd invited her out on
a date.

Her pulse had taken flight. He was so tall, so hand-some, so enigmatic, so different from any other man she'd ever met. Man and earth combined in Shane. He was everything she'd fantasized about as a young girl.

She'd said yes immediately, thrilled to know he was interested in her as a woman, not as an heiress. She'd had enough of expectations and she'd longed to live her life in her own way. Shane was part of her new life.

She recalled their fourth date. Shane had taken her to the county fair, where he'd given her the aspen leaf, a gift that meant more than all her fancy jewelry simply because he'd wanted her to have it.

She remembered his heart-stoppingly romantic pro-posal, their midsummer wedding beneath the sun and trees, the thrill and fear of wondering if she was preg-nant, then...

Nothing.

Warm air whispered from the floor vents, but that couldn't stop goose bumps from sliding up and down her arms. It was winter now, meaning she'd lost at least a couple of months. So what had happened that was so bad between then and now?

He said their argument couldn't be fixed, and yet...

Was it possible her memory loss was a blessing?

She continued to hold the aspen leaf—a promise of forever—close to her heart.

Maybe, with nothing to hold back her true emotions, her honesty could find Shane's heart.

Angie was nothing if not a strong and determined woman. And now she had a mission, getting her husband back.

After gingerly climbing from bed, she grabbed the post, waiting for the world to right itself.

She slid into her undergarments slowly, then pulled

on the sweatpants and shirt, and borrowed a pair of his thick socks from a drawer before moving into the living room, toward her future.

Shane stared out the window and she moved up behind him. Hardhat, the adorable Labrador, cocked his head to one side. One ear flopped over endearingly. She smiled. At least the dog didn't mind having her here.

Before she reached Shane, he turned, facing her with a formidable frown.

The hand she'd been reaching toward him fell to her side.

"You should be in bed."

"Only if you'll join me."

The frown deepened. "Angie," he warned.

"I want to know where I stand with you. Do you want a divorce?" Despite her best efforts, emotion ran her words together into a breathless blur. "I don't think I could bear that."

"It's too late for that discussion," he stated flatly.

"Don't you want me?"

He dragged a hand through his hair, pulling strands back from his face and emphasizing the fine lines grooved beside dark green eyes.

Frightened of the answer but needing to know, she asked, "Is that it? You don't find me desirable anymore?"

His gaze swept up her, holding nothing back. He lingered at the swell of her breasts, looking at her for a long, long time, long enough for her nipples to tighten with want.

"Hell, Ang, a man would have to be blind to not want you."

"Did you kick me out of the house?"

"No."

"Then I left you."

Silence roared.

"Yes."

Terror tapped a staccato in her veins. "But I'd never do that, not after what your mother did."

"Wouldn't you?"

She shuddered. All of a sudden, she was no longer certain of anything. "Why? Why would I do that to you? To Sarah? To us?"

"You were playing house with a poor boy and decided you didn't like it. Your future with a social equal was more important than your sworn promise to me."

She shook her head. "It's not possible. I don't believe it, Shane, I can't."

"I've got your note, Angie."

"Note?"

"A Dear John letter. An excuse, no apology."

From the other room, the teakettle shrilled. She seized the opportunity to escape him, fleeing into the kitchen.

Her hand shook as she turned off the burner.

Collapsing against the counter, she gulped half a dozen desperate breaths.

She'd left him?

Her heart raced and the aspen leaf lay against it, suddenly feeling cold. Tears swelled in her eyes. She was confused, vulnerable, and she hated not being in control.

Shane entered the room, curving his hands around her shoulders reassuringly. "I shouldn't have told you."

"I'm fine," she lied. "I'll bring you some tea in a minute."

"Forget the tea." Releasing one hand, he held a finger beneath her eye and transferred the moisture from her lashes to his skin, as if trying to take away her pain.

He held her gaze as captive as he held her tear. With his thumb, he stroked the dampness until it disappeared.

How was it possible that the love they shared had vanished? Nothing was more important to her than Shane.

When she'd accepted his proposal, she'd turned her back on her family and the groom her father had chosen for her. She'd known the consequences—being disinherited and cut off from her family—and was willing to pay the price because the idea of a future without Shane's love hurt even more.

There had to be something he didn't know, something she couldn't remember. She was still the same woman who promised to love Shane forever. "I wouldn't have willingly destroyed our relationship."

She tried to pull away, only to have Shane once again tighten his grip.

"The doctor said you need to rest. I'll see to it that you do."

She laughed, a brittle sound. "That's the only reason you didn't throw me out in the snow, isn't it? Because the doctor said I'm your responsibility."

"Don't."

"You must hate me."

"Hate? No."

"But you don't care."

"I've had time to get over it."

"Over me?"

His silence spoke louder than words.

"Go in the front room and curl up in front of the fire," he said into the crackling silence.

She didn't.

He pulled her a little closer, so close she inhaled the

scent of masculine determination and saw the flash of daring in his eyes. He overwhelmed her.

"Go willingly, or I'll carry you there myself."

"I'll make my own decisions—"

"You always have. No matter who you hurt."

She flinched.

"I'm not negotiable, Angie. Don't push me."

Her heart was as heavy as the snow suffocating the outdoors. Needing to regroup, she conceded. For now.

She lowered her gaze, and he released her.

Crossing to the couch, she massaged her shoulders where he'd held her.

Hardhat jumped up beside her. Absently she ran her hand down his back. With a sound that was half yawn, half whine, he dropped his head in her lap.

She looked at the beautiful stone fireplace, and a cold frisson frosted her spine. Their wedding picture used to occupy the center of the mantel. Now it was bare.

Shane brought in two cups of tea and put them on coasters. "Hardhat's not allowed on the couch."

"Sorry."

"He figures you're a soft touch."

"I don't know him."

"No."

She exhaled shakily. "And the furniture?"

"I bought it after you left."

"You've made other changes, too. You've added on, put in lots of windows. It doesn't look like a cabin any longer. It's more like one of those fabulous mountain retreats you'd see in a magazine. It takes a while to make those kind of changes."

He nodded in agreement.

"How long, Shane? How long have I been gone?"

He crouched to scratch Hardhat behind one ear. "It doesn't matter."

Despite herself, she reached for him, curving her fingers around his shoulder. In the craziness, he was her only anchor. Damn it, she needed him. Her voice hoarse, she whispered, "It matters to me."

He looked at her squarely. "Five years. You left me over five years ago."

She gasped. Not months, but years. *Years of her life had vanished.*

Instantly he covered her hand with his.

Something in her stomach, warm and deep, fluttered. No matter what had happened, she still responded to his most casual touch. "I want to see the letter."

He cursed beneath his breath. "I'm under strict orders from Dr. Johnson to keep you calm."

Her laugh was frayed at the edges. "Things can't be any worse than they already are."

He clamped his lips together.

"Let me see the letter. I have to know..."

"Sorry."

"It has to be real to me, Shane." She turned her palm up. "Please understand."

After long seconds, when she thought he'd refuse, he finally nodded curtly.

While he was gone, she wondered if she was making the right decision. Maybe it would make everything seem real, maybe her memory would flood back.

It didn't.

She didn't recognize the stationery. But there was no mistaking the word *Shane* in her handwriting.

The edges of the paper were tattered and yellowed, the creases crisp, as if he'd dragged a thumbnail across them with finality.

She paused before unfolding the page, meeting his gaze. It was as cold as the winter wind battering the cabin.

Her hand trembled as she held the letter, and the words blurred from the tears gathering in her eyes.

Shane strode away. His back to her, he tossed a log on the fire and stabbed the timber with a poker.

Shane,
I'm going home to my father. Don't try and find me. I don't want to see you again. Our marriage was a fling and a mistake.
 I never loved you.

           Angie.

The brutal coldness of the words sliced into her heart. "It's not true," she whispered, her voice shaking with unshed emotion.

How could she have done this to him? *Why* would she do this to him? It couldn't have been that she'd fallen out of love with him, not with the emotion still swelling in her soul.

"I loved you then," she said. "I love you now."

Shane said nothing.

There had to be an explanation, and now, more than ever, she was desperate to know what had happened to the five years erased by an accident.

"Did we have a fight? Is that why I wrote this?" she asked softly, the words breaking on a sob.

"No." He turned to face her. "I went to work. We'd made love...."

His gaze skimmed up and down her body, and she felt it like a caress. A blush colored her face as recognition flared into need.

"Being with you made me late for work. I didn't mind. You'd almost convinced me to call in sick and stay in bed with you."

"Did you wish you had?"

"At first."

"And now?"

"If you didn't love me, I'd rather you left. Like cauterizing a wound. Hurts like hell in the beginning. Less painful in the end."

"Did you come after me?"

"Yeah. But not at first. About a month after the divorce was final, I was out with Slade Birmingham." Beside Shane, the fire devoured the dried wood, hissing and crackling.

"I had a few to drink. Before that I'd refused to grab the bottle like my old man used to do." He jammed his hands into his front pockets. His eyes, electrified by the fire, burned into hers. "That night, Angie, the pain caught up with me. It was my birthday, the anniversary of my mom walking out."

Oh, God, oh, God, why had she asked? His pain cut through her, and her abdomen constricted.

"I drove all the way to Chicago, like a lovesick fool." She winced.

"Arrived just in time for your wedding reception."

Her jaw went slack. "My..."

"Wedding reception. After your marriage to Jack Hague." Shane's eyes darkened like a storm in the forest.

"No," she protested, disbelief rocketing through her. She wouldn't have married Jack, even if it was the only thing her father had ever expected of her.

"Oh, yeah. In a long white gown, diamonds in your ears, huge vases of white flowers everywhere, a band, champagne, a sit-down meal… all the things I wanted to give you and couldn't. The things that apparently mattered to you, even though you said they didn't.''

A headache threatened to split her skull.

"Six months after you sneaked out of my life. The ink was barely dry on our divorce papers, Angie. *It was as if we'd never happened.*"

Maybe he was right; maybe she would have been better off not knowing.

"Your daddy figured out who I was and escorted me outside. He was kind enough to answer a few questions for me. He explained you really hadn't come to live in Colorado, that spending the summer with your aunt was something to give you a taste of the real world, nothing more.''

"No. That's not true. I came to Colorado to get away, to be an independent woman.''

"Your father said when you were done playing house with a man who wasn't your social equal, you called him and begged him to bail you out. You were tired of being broke, tired of being a surrogate mother to my sister.''

Her head swam. "No. I loved Sarah.''

"Not only that, but in the generous spirit of the celebration, he wrote out a ten thousand dollar check to ensure I never contacted you again.'' His words were short and bitter. "I tore it up and threw the pieces at his feet. Didn't need money to stay the hell out of your life.'' His tone dropped another octave. "It would have cost him more than that to make me speak to you again.''

"And now I'm back.''

"And when your memory returns, I'll have a few questions for you.''

"Like...?"

He shoved his hands even deeper into his pockets. To keep them to himself?

"For starters, are you still married? Are you Angie Hague? Oh, wait, maybe it'd be *Angela* Hague."

She pressed her hand to her temples. "Shane, please..."

"Does he still have a claim on you? And if he does, why the hell are you sleeping in my bed?"

Four

The world reeled and she couldn't even take a breath. She was in love with Shane, only Shane. The idea of another man touching her, holding her, making love to her...

"No," she whispered. Desperately she looked at her left hand. "I'm not wearing a ring." And there was no indentation where one might have rested.

"That doesn't mean anything."

"No other man has any claim on me. I never wanted anyone but you."

"Stop, Angie. I've had enough of your lies."

She clutched the aspen leaf. "It wasn't a lie."

He stared at her, long and deep. She scrambled to her unsteady feet, reaching for the couch for support. Blinded by tears, she headed for the door.

"Where the hell are you going?"

"I've got to know." She reached the entryway before

he did and yanked her jacket and purse from the hook where he'd hung them.

Dropping to her knees, she jerked open her purse and dumped it upside down.

In an instant, he was kneeling in front of her, grabbing her shoulders and forcing her to look at him. "Angie..."

Shrugging off his grip, she dug through the cosmetics, gum wrappers and checkbook, then snatched up her wallet, desperately searching for pieces of her past.

There were no pictures in her wallet, no snapshots of her and Jack.

Her fingers trembled as she pulled out her Illinois driver's license.

Angela Burton.

Her name was listed as Angela Burton...her maiden name.

She let go of a breath she hadn't realized she was holding, then studied her credit cards and checkbook.

She looked at Shane.

His eyes were narrowed, and a wary mixture of anger and concern played across green depths.

"I'm Angela Burton."

He curved a hand around her wrist. "So it says."

A pain ripped through her and she reached her free hand toward him, tracing her finger down his familiar, yet so different, shadowed cheek.

A thousand questions swamped her mind. Why was she in Colorado? Why was she at his house? Why did she think they were still in love? How could she have left him?

She'd never met anyone like him. Tender, protective, arrogant, maddening, passionate, they'd shared dozens of emotions, each time growing a little closer.

Grief, a sharp, stabbing pain, shot through her. She'd

left him, walked out on him in the coldest, most callous way possible. She'd done what his mother and Delilah had done, after swearing she wouldn't. Angie had betrayed their love, and she *didn't know why*.

No wonder he didn't like her, didn't want her. "I'm sorry, Shane, so, so sorry."

"For leaving or coming back?"

"Both."

"It's a little late for that, isn't it?"

He released her wrist, and she dropped her license. "I'm not married to him."

"No?"

"I'd know it if I were."

"Would you? How? How do you know anything, Angie?"

She looked at him with wide-eyed innocence, something he no longer believed in.

Protectively, she curled her fingers around the dulled aspen leaf. "If I hadn't loved you, why would I have kept the only gift you ever gave me?"

"Good question, since you didn't keep your wedding ring."

When she opened her eyes, they were wide, and the irises were ringed with a deep, haunted blue.

Regret pulsed in Shane. He was under doctor's orders to keep her calm, not badger her. Her face was pale, and her lower lip trembled.

There was something about her...something that he instinctively responded to, making him want to care for her. That much had never changed.

She'd always dragged deep emotion from him, even when he'd tried to bury it, like he'd buried his past. Not satisfied with that, with his promises of love and trust, Angie had asked for even more. They'd argued about

the part of his heart that he'd tried to hold back. She'd
wanted all of him, even the parts that he despised. And
that made it all the more difficult when he learned she'd
never even cared.

And now, even though the doctor gave him instruc-
tions, Shane had a hard time following them. When he'd
gone to the bedroom to get her Dear John letter and seen
their wedding rings beside it, her smaller one nestled in
his much larger one, the past and the pain he'd stuffed
away had gusted through him.

No other woman possessed that power over him.

And he didn't like it. It'd be easier if he was indif-
ferent. But damn it all, he wasn't.

Guilt gnawed at him, making him wish he'd kept his
mouth shut. He should have kept her calm, waited for
the roads to clear, then sent her on her way. He might
have saved himself a hell of a lot of irritation.

Instead, they knelt near each other, close, but no
longer touching, Hardhat looking at them with his head
cocked to one side and wind hammering at the door.

"Look," he said. "I'm sorry."

"You're sorry?" she echoed.

"How about a truce?"

"So you can stop worrying about me?"

He shook his head. "We can't change the past. We
can't go anywhere until the roads are cleared, and the
phone is dead. We might as well accept it."

"Be polite strangers."

"Yeah."

"I don't know if I can do that, Shane. My past is a
blur and I can't believe I would have walked out on you,
no matter what. And marrying Jack Hague? I barely
liked the man. I know my daddy wanted me to marry
Jack because of the merger, but I married you instead."

When he started to say something, she plowed on.

"I don't even have a present, let alone a future. I don't know why I'm here, if I live in Chicago." She exhaled. "Maybe I came to see my aunt Emma. Maybe she's expecting me?"

"I doubt it. Miss Starr's last gossip column said Emma Kelsey's spending the winter in Florida."

She squeezed her eyes shut. "I should have known that."

"Angie, getting worked up isn't going to help your memory come back. You owe it to yourself to relax."

"I'm not sure I know how."

"That hasn't changed, then, either." He smiled, then held up a hand. "I don't mean anything by that, honest. Truce?"

"Do I have a choice?"

"You can fight..."

"But I'd never win?"

He stood and offered his hand. She took it, and her fingers were icy cold, despite the cabin's warmth. He didn't want to feel sympathy for her, but there it was. She needed him.

He led her back to his bedroom. "You take my bed."

"That's not right. I'll sleep in Sarah's room."

"She took all her bedding to college. I never got around to shopping for new stuff."

"Another thing that hasn't changed," she said. "Do you remember looking for towels at the general store? You grabbed the first pile you saw."

"Didn't figure there was any sense in reading labels when you were just going to use it for ten seconds a day."

Something pulsed between them. She'd bought a couple of nice-quality towels, telling him there was a difference in the absorbency and the way it felt against skin. Later, he'd experimented on her bare back, then dragged the cotton lower, working it on her thighs and making her squirm.... "Take the bedroom. I'll sleep on the couch. I'll hear you if you need anything."

"I don't like being an unwanted responsibility."

"Take the bedroom, Ang."

"But—"

"You can't win."

"I'll pay you back for this. Somehow."

"Forget it. Call it western hospitality. I'd do the same for any neighbor."

"But you did it for me."

Her words played in his head long after she'd closed the door behind her.

After feeding Hardhat and turning the thermostat up a couple of degrees, Shane grabbed a pillow and blanket from the linen closet.

The couch was too short, the fireplace crackled too loudly, the wind drove sheets of snow against the cabin, all making it impossible for Shane to sleep.

Or that's what he told himself.

In reality, every time he closed his eyes, he pictured Angie. He saw her struggling through the blizzard to reach him, trust and love etched in her features. He saw the way her face fell when he'd told her their relationship couldn't be saved. And he saw the way she'd reached for him with womanly desire when she'd woken from her nap. All the images had something in common: Angie's innocence. That was all an act, a lie, he reminded himself.

Funny, he'd never thought she was that good an actress.

Hardhat made funny doggy noises as he made himself

more comfortable in front of the fire. Shane hadn't known it was possible to be envious of a dog. Hardhat just accepted people for who they were, expected to be loved, then slept contentedly.

Shane should be so lucky.

What was that old saying? No rest for the wicked? Maybe that's why she'd been in bed half the night without sleeping a wink.

She sat up and pulled Shane's pillow to her chest. That was as close as she was ever going to get to him again.

Was she wicked? Had she done something so unspeakably horrible to Shane without any reason? Was that why she'd blocked out the past five years?

Five years.

She felt like a whole person but knew she wasn't. Anything could happen in five years. Obviously a lot had.

Breath hitched in her throat. If what Shane said was true, she'd left him and walked straight into the dictatorial arms of a man she didn't even like, a man determined to run his life the same way he'd run his company.

But she wasn't wearing a ring. And her maiden name was listed on all her cards and identification.

For reassurance, she touched the aspen leaf, something she swore she'd wear always to remember Shane's love. Her wedding ring had meant the world to her, but the inexpensive trinket had meant more.

He'd invited her to the county fair and she'd pretended not to notice how buying the piece of jewelry had wiped out his last dollar. She'd never meant that much to a man. Her father, while he loved her and raised her after her mother's death, had seen her as an asset to his company and goals. Before she'd met Shane, Jack had seen her as a mean to his ends, as well. Shane, though, had seen her simply as a woman.

She wasn't blind to his faults, knowing he was as demanding in his own way as her father had always been, but she'd admired Shane. Most of the men she went to college with were obsessed with partying and accumulating possessions.

In his early twenties, Shane was running his own business, trusting his gut instinct and working his behind off. His father had died when Shane was nineteen and Sarah was only eleven. Rather than letting the state take his sister away, Shane fought for her, supported her, raised her.

Shane hadn't been a thing like any other man she knew. He didn't own a suit, let alone a tux. He wore blue jeans and boots and bought his sunglasses at the discount department store in Durango. He drove a seen-better-days pickup truck and didn't lust after a fancy sports car.

Knowing Shane had illuminated her life, and she'd seen how shallow other men were.

Working that summer more than five years ago had taught Angie a lot about life. She didn't want to be a woman who was spoiled and pampered. She wanted to make a difference.

Could she truly have changed that much? Could she have become one of the people who had seemed so shallow?

The holes in her memory making her restless, she tossed aside Shane's pillow and burrowed beneath the blankets only to push them back when thoughts of Shane shamelessly snuggled alongside her.

Being in this room, in his bed, reminded her of the first time they'd made love, his shock at finding her a virgin and the way he'd gently eased into her.

Now, as vividly as if it were yesterday, she heard his softly encouraging words, recalled the feel of him entering, stretching her, the sharp pain, then later, the thrill as he'd brought her to the edge.

Tossing the blanket and comforter aside, she jumped from the bed.

Her feet touched the cool hardwood flooring and the world tipped the wrong way, a nasty reminder of her accident. She couldn't stay in this room, between his sheets. Deciding a cup of tea might help settle her nerves, she found a flannel shirt, but paused before putting it on. At one time she wouldn't have thought twice about wearing his clothes, but now...

Still, he was asleep, she hoped. But in case he woke up, she didn't want to be caught in only a T-shirt and panties.

She cracked the door and peeked out, her heart hammering. By the firelight, she saw the rhythmic rise and fall of his chest. Hardhat roused, and she froze near the couch. With a yawn and a stretch, the dog followed her.

From the kitchen, she hazarded a nervous glance in Shane's direction, then exhaled softly when she saw he hadn't been disturbed.

Running water gushed like a waterfall in the stainless steel sink as she filled the kettle. Setting it on the stove, she turned the burner on high.

Hardhat nudged his empty water bowl, then, when she didn't respond right away, pawed it until it turned over with a solid clunk.

"He's good at getting what he wants."

She jumped and slowly spun.

So much for hoping he'd stay asleep.

Her breath seemed to wobble in her lungs. Her sensual images, combined with the oh-so-sexy reality of him made it impossible to breathe.

Casually, he leaned one shoulder against the wall. His hips were cocked to one side, his dark T-shirt was untucked and alluringly rumpled, his jeans were softly wrinkled and his feet were bare. "Couldn't sleep?" he asked.

"Thought I'd have the tea I didn't get earlier."

"Me, neither," he said, honesty cutting through her defenses.

She braced herself near the sink.

"I heard you get out of bed, then heard you open the door and walk in here."

"But I tiptoed."

"Yeah. I know."

Hardhat pushed his dish closer to her. Grateful for something to do, she picked it up. When she'd filled the bowl, she bent to put it on the floor, then froze when she stood up and met Shane's gaze.

No longer cold, his eyes were warm, shooting a molten sensation through her. "Would you like a cup of tea? There's enough water for both of us," she said breathlessly, unable to separate the Angie who still loved him from the Angela who'd left him.

She prayed he'd refuse, hoped he wouldn't.

"You paused by the couch."

"Because Hardhat got up."

"Is that the only reason?"

"Yes."

He said nothing.

"No," she admitted reluctantly but truthfully.

"You wear the same perfume."

"Chanel No. 5."

"But you don't use the same shampoo."

"You've noticed?"

"Angie, I've noticed every damn thing about you since you got here."

She folded her arms across her middle, then forced herself to relax when she realized she'd dragged her clothes a couple of inches up her thighs.

The teakettle shrilled. She hoped it would shatter the intimacy, but it didn't.

She dropped a tea bag in a mug, then splashed hot water over it, pretending he wasn't there.

"Tell me why you couldn't sleep," he said, dragging a chair away from the table, then sprawling on the seat.

At first glance, he appeared relaxed. Then she realized there was nothing casual about him. His right hand was on the table, curled into a fist. His right foot was planted on the hardwood floor and his spine rested rigidly against the chair's back. He could be on his feet in a fraction of a second.

"Tell me," he repeated softly.

She took honey from a cupboard and drizzled it in her cup, rather than giving the bottle a good squeeze.

"You're stalling," he said.

She put down the honey bear, but stayed where she was, halfway across the kitchen from him. Safer that way.

With the toes of his left foot, he pushed another chair away from the table in silent invitation. He was still waiting.

Her heart hadn't stopped pounding since he walked in the room, and now it hammered even harder. "I don't know how to act," she admitted, reluctantly taking the seat across from him. They were too close, she was too aware of his broad chest, the sinews of his forearms, the hurt in his eyes.

"I couldn't sleep because I was thinking of you," he said. "I don't want to remember the good times."

"For me, they happened yesterday. I'm the same woman who loved you, but somehow I must be the same woman who left you. I can't believe that I feel this way about you if I walked out back then."

Leaning closer to him, she said, "I was thinking of that night we went to the county fair and you gave me this aspen leaf. My dad gave me a Jaguar for my high school graduation, but I walked away from that. This," she said, curling her hand around the pendant, "was why I walked away."

His brows drew together skeptically.

"I know you don't believe me. But I'll tell you this much, Shane. If I could turn back the clock to that day, I'd make sure you knew I loved you."

"Love isn't enough."

She had to ask, didn't want to, but she had to know... Licking her lips, she asked, "Is there someone else for you? Is that why you stopped me from touching you?"

"No. I stopped you before we ended up making love."

She glanced at him through half-lowered, shy lids. "But what if I wanted that, too?"

"That's not fair to either of us. You don't have a memory, and I have enough for both of us. I hope I have enough integrity not to take advantage of you."

She quickly stood. Her head spun and the world wobbled. Shane was there in an instant, holding her tight. Desperately she grabbed a fistful of his T-shirt, feeling the solidness of him and breathing in his scent.

"You okay?"

"I keep forgetting about my accident."

Something pulsed, something honest and pure. "Me, too," he said softly.

She didn't know how it happened, didn't question it, didn't try to stop it.

She responded completely to his kiss, holding nothing back.

The first touch of his tongue to hers made her knees weaken. He pressed a palm against the curve of her spine and, with the other hand, supported her neck. Her own hands crept higher, wrapping around him. She dug her fingers into the midnight darkness of his hair and pulled him in closer.

Moments later he deepened the kiss.

She couldn't think, and nothing mattered except for the fact she was in his arms, where she belonged.

Slowly he ended the kiss, pulling back and holding her at a distance until she regained her equilibrium. She pressed trembling fingers against her swollen lips.

"Go to bed," he said again, this time hoarsely. "And for heaven's sake, lock the door."

Five

What had he ever done to deserve this kind of torture?

Yesterday he'd had all the answers and his life was neatly compartmentalized. He worked all day, building his firm. In his spare time, he worked on the house. He got on with his life, content without love or emotional entanglements. No complications, just the way he liked it.

Until she barged in.

Now blood thrummed, demanding a release.

The storm must have frozen his brain cells. That was the only possible explanation for him kissing her, holding her, caring about her.

The bedroom door closed and locked. Mercifully.

Hardhat, after cocking his head to one side, abandoned his master and went into the living room, stretching his canine body in front of the hearth.

Shane dragged a hand through his hair.

Five years ago, Shane promised himself he'd never have her in his arms again. That intention had lasted right up until he had the chance.

The storm still snarled outside, and the only thing that was melting was his resolve to punish her for the sin of leaving him.

He'd claimed her lips and her responsiveness had chipped away at his hardened heart. And in that instant, the fact that she would inevitably walk out on him again didn't matter.

The woman sleeping in his room wasn't the same one who'd left him. Five years ago, she'd been head-turningly pretty. But now her face had character, little lines that spoke of hurt, but also compassion, and her lips were fuller, more inviting.

Older, more mature, more sure of herself, she intrigued him. Her eyes were deeper, bluer, and life's experiences lingered there.

He shouldn't care about anything but getting her healed and on her way.

But he did.

Damn it, he did.

Standing under the shower's hot spray, Angie tried to forget last night's wonderful kiss.

She opened her eyes, wanting to banish the images. It didn't work. She hadn't been able to escape him in sleep, couldn't do it in the shower.

She lathered and rinsed her hair, wincing when she accidentally rubbed the cut on her forehead. At least the pain was a reality check, reminding her of what she'd lost.

Angie stayed in the shower until the hot water heater had nearly run out. Then she spent the next half hour getting dressed, fully aware that this was his masculine domain. It bore his presence, his damp towel, his razor, everything that was personal and intimate.... She dried her hair and tried to ignore the sounds he made and the scent of freshly brewed coffee.

Finally, deciding she was an adult and that she could pretend the kiss hadn't happened, she joined him in the kitchen.

Hardhat ambled over to be petted, and Shane slowly turned, coffee mug in hand, hip leaning against the counter. The top two buttons on his shirt were unfastened, and she saw a scattering of darkly matted chest hair in the opening. "Morning," he said, his voice rough with a sexy scratch.

Her heart missed a beat.

Last night's abandoned mug sat on the table, instantly taking her back to the intimacy they'd shared, despite her decision to pretend it never happened. Hardhat nudged her with his nose and she dutifully scratched behind his ears.

"Phones are still out," Shane said. "Snow's still falling and blowing, and I haven't heard a plow."

She swallowed deeply. "So you're stuck with me for even longer."

"At least another day."

She didn't know what to think, how to react. "Are you hungry?" she asked, desperate to find something to do that would dispel the knot of tension in her stomach. She figured if she stayed busy, thoughts of her honest response couldn't haunt her.

"You offering to cook?"

"It's only fair." She crossed the kitchen and opened the freezer.

"What are you looking for?"

"Frozen fruit…strawberries, blueberries, something on that line."

"Unless Sarah's home on break, this is a bachelor pad."

He was right. Two boxes of premade pizza, a package of hot dogs, a pound of hamburger meat, a couple of steaks and a tray of ice cubes were the only things in the freezer. She nibbled on her lower lip. "Do you have eggs?"

"Yep. And milk and potatoes. Maybe some ham from the deli."

"Can I hope for baking powder?"

He opened a cupboard and emerged victorious. "Sometimes Sarah gets cravings for sweets."

He hooked a foot in front of the other and watched, interestedly. "What are you making?"

"Crepes." Aware of him intently watching her every motion, she asked, "Never seen a woman cook before?"

"Not you."

"But I'm a good cook."

"You didn't used to be."

She exhaled slowly, trying to think, getting a headache and finally sighing in frustration.

"Must be another talent of yours that I don't know about."

"There must be a lot we don't know about each other," she said.

"Guess we're learning."

The air around her sizzled, making it difficult to breathe. Concentrate, she told herself. Breakfast. "Will you slice some ham into thin pieces?"

She drizzled the batter into a hot frying pan and quickly rotated it to form the thin pancake. She had to reach in front of him for the plate of ham, and Shane didn't move out of her way, unnerving her. "Do you want to set the table?"

"Am I making you nervous?"

"No." She looked over her shoulder. "Yes."

He chuckled softly but said nothing.

She should have been unable to relax with him half-way across the room. Maybe if a renegade part of her didn't yearn to throw herself into his arms and unbutton the rest of his shirt the way she used to, it might have been easier.

Finally, the crepes made, she carried the skillet to the table.

"What do you take in your coffee?" he asked.

"I'm not sure."

He poured her a cup of coffee, added cream and sugar, then offered her the handle. Their fingers glanced off each other's. Then their eyes met. As if a match had been held close, something flared in the rich, green depths of his.

"I'm not sorry for kissing you last night."

So much for pretending it never happened. She looked away quickly.

"Are you?" he pressed.

"How could I be?" she asked softly, taking the cup and putting it down before she spilled it all over herself. She sat down, then wished she'd chosen another spot when he pulled out the chair right next to hers. "It's what I wanted."

"What if I were to do it again?"

"Given how you feel about me..." She looked at him and honestly said, "And how I still feel about you, you were right to stop it before it went any further."

Now that he'd mentioned the kiss, every nerve ending was on alert and her blood hummed in her veins. She was aware of him, and in her mind, they'd only made love yesterday. But inviting intimacy was asking for trouble when her memory returned, when he saw her as the woman who'd left him.

They ate in silence, and Angie was unable to swallow more than a few bites.

"You were right," he said. "You are a good cook."

After scraping her leftovers into a very happy Hardhat's bowl, she offered to clean the rest of the kitchen if he washed the dishes.

It only took her a few minutes to realize she should have sent him away instead of asking for help.

Their bodies touched several times when she carried dishes to the sink, and her insides leaped with awareness.

He rolled back his sleeves to reveal dark hair and tanned skin.

She caught his scent, that of the mountains and untamed power. Years of hard, physical work had honed his body to muscular tightness. "Do you still have your firm?" she asked, more to distract herself than anything else.

How little she knew him now, but how well her body remembered him.

He nodded as he dried the frying pan. "Masters Construction is alive and well. I don't get on-site as much as I'd like. I'm too busy running the place."

"So you have employees now?"

"A dozen or so."

"I always knew you'd be a success."

"Did you?"

"I could feel it," she admitted. "I knew a lot of men who were content to coast through life, driving the cars and joining the clubs their fathers had earned for them. But you... I admired your determination, your dedication to Sarah. I knew you'd be the best at whatever you wanted to do.''

He looked as though he was going to say something, but then changed his mind. He stacked a plate on top of another.

"And Sarah—how's she?" She was rambling, but better that than noticing the way their fingers touched every time he took a dish from her.

"Getting good grades. First person in the family to go to college. I'm proud of her."

"You should be."

"She used to ask about you."

Angie looked at him, startled. Finally finished with the dishes, she pulled the stopper from the drain and dried her hands on a kitchen towel.

"She looked up to you. She never knew her mother, and she liked that you cared."

"I did. I still do."

"Sarah missed you almost as much as I did."

Her heart twisted again. She and Sarah had been close. Angie and Shane even took her on a few of their dates rather than leaving her home alone. Sometimes Shane had wanted a break from raising his sister, but Angie had rarely minded Sarah's company.

As an only child, Angie appreciated Sarah's uncon-ditional love. And in leaving, Angie had destroyed that, too. Just what had her actions cost him and his family? "I'm sorry," she whispered, laying her hand on his, then squeezing gently.

"Angie—"

She rose on tiptoes, not thinking beyond the moment, and threaded her hands around his neck. "I'm sorry," she said again. "For everything." As atonement, she kissed him. At first, he didn't react, then he kissed her back, his tongue tasting, testing hers. Within seconds, he took over, deepening the kiss as he explored her responses.

Leaning her against the sink, he maneuvered them so his hand could cup her breast.

Heat flooded downward from her stomach, and she softly said, "Yes."

He snagged the hem of her T-shirt and drew it off, ending the kiss long enough to pull the cotton over her head. Cool air hit her skin, only to be replaced by his warm hands.

Her knees weakened, and he caught her, sweeping her from her feet and carrying her into the living room. Their eyes met and held for a second as he placed her on the couch. He knelt on the floor, facing her.

His gaze swept up her body, lingering on her breasts, barely covered by her lacy bra.

Here, now, at least his icy veneer had cracked. Maybe, with time, she could melt it entirely.

"Make love to me."

"Angie—"

"I know what I'm doing, what I'm asking for. Make love to me, Shane."

With his thumb, he stroked her lip. She opened her mouth and caught his thumb, curling her tongue around it and sucking.

He groaned.

Eyes closed, Angie leaned forward again, burying her hands in the thickness of his hair.

His mind resisted, wondering what the hell he was doing, thinking of making love to his ex-wife, but his body responded as it always had.

Lack of desire had never been a problem between

them. From the moment their fingers had first touched when they'd shaken hands to the instant their bodies had joined on their wedding night, sparks had arced between them.

And now the warmth of her tongue curled around him, and the gentle sucking reminded him of the past, when he'd believed she was made for his arms, his bed, his body.

Seared by heat, a log shattered in the fireplace.

"Angie..."

She reached for him and pressed her hand to the front of his jeans. Pleasure gusted deep in his loins. She was a seductress, turning him on in ways he couldn't imagine. Want coiled into demand.

No, this bold woman wasn't the same one he'd married. She was willing to ask for what she wanted and needed. Greedily he wanted to know *her*.

She fumbled with the buttons on his shirt, then dragged the flannel from his waistband.

Suddenly he couldn't get enough of her.

He moved forward, spreading her thighs, and she reached for his belt buckle, unhooking it. With a hiss matched by the fireplace, the leather slid from its denim loops, and metal clanked on the floor.

A pink, frothy confection was the only thing covering her breasts. He traced the skin above the lacy cups of her bra. Her head fell forward until her chin all but rested on her chest, near the golden aspen leaf. A small sound, somewhere between need and a sigh, escaped from her partially opened lips.

A small bow rested at the front clasp of the bra, the tied piece of satin making him think of a gift begging to be opened.

Savoring each second, he parted the fabric and shucked the straps from her shoulders.

Her breasts spilled forward and he caught them in his cupped palms, holding, feeling, testing her feminine weight.

"Shane!"

He brushed his thumbs across her nipples. They hardened and grew, and she cried out.

She was the same woman, and so much more.

Pinching the tiny buds between his thumb and forefinger, he watched her reaction. Honest emotions tripped across her face. Her brows drew together and her eyelids sealed off the vibrant color of her blue eyes. She smiled, then it faded to a gasp when he rolled his fingers. "Stop?" he asked.

"No...it's..."

Gently he squeezed the distended nipples once more. "Tell me," he urged.

"Incredible." She pressed herself forward, against him, wordlessly seeking more.

That he still possessed this power over her shot raw pleasure through him.

He stood and then pulled her up.

She looked at him through hazy blue eyes. He recalled seeing that haze in her eyes when he made love to her the first time, when he learned it had been her first time ever. She'd been saving herself for someone special. For him, she'd confessed.

Five years ago, like now, blood had thundered in him, demolishing every thought but that of being inside her. "I want to see you. All of you."

He unzipped her pants. His urges gnawing at him, he watched as she wriggled the denim past her hips, then down her thighs. In seconds she was wearing only a pair of panties—and not the sensible cotton type he remembered. These were pink, barely there....

He sucked in a shallow breath. "You're lovely."

A piece of wood in the hearth popped.

He couldn't wait a moment longer.

He undressed as she shimmied out of her panties.

Sitting on the couch, he pulled her on top of him, her thighs straddling his. "I want to watch you."

"Good, that way I can watch you, too." She smiled, a secretive smile that walloped him in the gut.

Placing one hand on her spine, he angled downward till he found the small of her back. With gentle pressure, he encouraged her to sit up straight.

When she was positioned the way he wanted, he placed one hand in the rich tangle of her hair, cradling her head.

Her fingers curled around him, as if she never wanted to let him go. He lowered his head, laving his tongue across the tip of her breast.

She shivered; he shuddered.

Shane suckled her breast, cupping her nipple with his tongue and drawing her deeper into his mouth.

Angie wriggled, her body moving rhythmically on his thighs.

Her head pressed against his palm as her back arched. In answer to her unspoken demand, he increased the pressure on her breast, then moved one hand between her legs, finding her most sensitive spot.

Her fingers dug deeper into his shoulders as their rocking motion became more intense.

His fingers slipped against her dampness, and he gently inserted one finger into her, then another.

"Shane!"

He pressed the pad of his thumb against her, then stroked her once, then again with even more pressure.

She gasped.

Shane enjoyed hearing her ragged breathing, the sound of his name hanging in the air, then the way she whimpered as she collapsed against him.

Her arms went around him, and instinctively he held her. A fine sheen of moisture clung to her nape beneath the curtain of her hair.

Slowly her breathing returned to normal. And so did his.

After long moments, she leaned back. She reached a hand out, tracing down his unshaven cheek, drawing a finger across his eyebrow.

Her eyes were wide with wonder and excitement.

"I want to make you feel what I just felt, Shane," she said, tangling her hand in the mat of hair on his chest. She smoothed her palm across him, finding his nipples and gently scraping her fingernails across them.

He sucked in a breath.

Triumphantly she smiled.

Then she moved back, a couple of inches away from him, and cupped her hand around him.

Blood surged through him. As she moved higher, he grew against her palm. She squeezed gently and he bit back a groan.

"Fill me," she said.

He did.

Lifting her hips, he settled her near the tip of his manhood. Her gaze never leaving his, she gripped his shoulders for support and lowered herself. He felt her body stretching to fit his, and her tightness made him struggle for control.

Finally she'd taken him in all the way, and she rested

for a moment, her knees sinking into the cushions, her thighs cradling his hips. Her arms were crossed behind his neck, and her full breasts were crushed against his chest. Woman to man, just as it should be.

Her hair draped across his chest as he'd fantasized, reminding him of a silken waterfall. He curled his hands into the strands, then let them sift through his fingers.

The fantasy wasn't as incredible as the reality of it, of her.

As if they'd made love yesterday and not five years ago, they moved in harmony, Angie's body meeting each of his insistent thrusts.

Need built, churning. She was close; he felt it. Arching up, he drove deeply, spilling himself inside her.

She continued to move, drawing more from him until he pulsed against her womb.

It was long moments until he could breathe normally. Slowly Angie leaned forward, wrapping her arms around his neck and gently kissing his temple. Her body was sweat-slickened and sexy, her fit around him was perfect.

Rationally he knew he might regret their lovemaking. But with Angie in his arms, this moment was the only thing that mattered.

"You've got goose bumps."

"I'm getting chilly," Angie admitted.

"Let me take you to bed, or we can move in front of the fireplace," he said, glancing up at her.

She licked her lower lip. "The fireplace." It was closer.

He reached for the Navajo throw on the back of the couch and tossed it onto the floor. Then he helped her untangle herself. She stood, but only for a second, before he scooped her off her feet again. At one time, he'd done that more figuratively, but with the same, heady effect on her.

He placed her on the throw, then smoothed it out and grabbed a pillow and plumped it behind her.

He moved between her legs, and she spread her thighs, inviting him in.

They'd made love dozens of times in the past, but Angie never recalled it being like this.

She was bolder, she realized, but Shane didn't seem to mind. He was different, too. He took her response and demanded more than he ever would have before. And that thrilled her. They moved together in perfect harmony, a give and take unlike any she'd ever known with him. And after it was over, he covered her with the blanket and cradled her. The covering of dark hair was downy soft, tempting her to explore.

But it was his face that made her lungs seem to shrink. His eyes were more moody than ever. Their rich depths now spoke of hurt and resolve. And in that instant, she knew she might have his body and his masculine response, but she'd never again have his heart.

In asking him to make love to her, she'd hoped for an emotional connection between them. But that was one thing he wasn't offering.

He fingered her hair tenderly, and she blinked back tears. This was impossible. Why couldn't she remember the past five years? Why had she believed she could make love with him and keep her heart separate from her body?

How was she ever going to survive this?

She'd left him once before. But surely that couldn't be as difficult as doing it a second time....

Six
___

"**M**orning," Shane said softly as Angie stirred against his chest. Just for a minute, he allowed himself to enjoy holding her. Then, quietly he added, "It stopped snowing."

Her hand tightened into a fist near his middle. "I guess they'll be able to get a snowplow out soon."

"Yeah." It would be for the best, he figured. She was getting close to him again, and that meant he was sliding into dangerous territory. Shane didn't much care for dangerous territory. "I need to shower."

He slowly disentangled their bodies, trying to ignore the noble part of him that wanted to reassure her.

Shane left her in the bed, grabbed some clothes, then spared a quick glance over his shoulder. She was rigid, the bedcovers pulled up to her chin. Her eyes were wide and the blue was frosted with unasked questions.

Tension gnawed in his gut. More powerful than sexual hunger, this emotion bit him.

He closed the bathroom door between them.

Even though she didn't recall seeing it before, she recognized the chilly expression that clouded his green eyes.

Yesterday was over. Today, if he could arrange it, she would be leaving.

The click of the door had sounded final.

She didn't know how she felt. Confused, mostly. Part of her wanted to stay. The part that had been exposed and was now vulnerable wanted to run.

Needing some sort of action, she got up and pulled on one of his cotton flannel shirts. She crossed to the window and stood there, listening to the water run in the shower and trying not to think about their incredible lovemaking.

She stared through the icy windowpane at the vast white landscape, broken only by towering ponderosa pines. The sun was shining, reflecting off the sparkling layer of snow crystals.

It looked as cold as her insides suddenly felt, and she shivered. The world lay silent and still, as if holding its breath.

Unconsciously she touched the golden aspen leaf that still hung around her neck. Had it been a talisman for the last five years? she wondered. Or had she put it on just before coming back to Colorado? And if she had, why?

She dropped her hands to her sides, more frustrated now by her lack of memory than she had been earlier, before they'd made love.

In the other room, the water stopped, and she heard

the glass door bang in its casing. Galvanized into action, she hurried to the closet, looking for the box where he kept the things she'd left behind. She didn't want to be half-naked when he came out of the bathroom.

She pulled out a box and dragged it into the bedroom, then opened the lid, expecting to find jeans and sweatshirts inside. Instead, she found her bridal bouquet.

Her breath nearly choked her.

One hand pressed to her throat, she reached toward the silk flower arrangement and traced her fingertips over the rose's pink petals. She remembered it and the dress she'd worn. She recalled the ceremony, of walking toward him on the arm of his friend and best man, Slade Birmingham. It might only have happened yesterday, so clearly did she see Shane's anxious smile and the wary set of his lips, as if he expected her to turn and run. She hadn't, at least not then.

Her hand shook as she moved the bouquet aside and took out their photo album. These were snapshots, not professional portraits. They couldn't afford a photographer, so a couple of friends had taken candid shots. The pictures were grainy, the colors watery, but her and Shane's expressions were indelibly etched.

There was Shane, kneeling in front of her. He'd lifted the hem of her dress to take off the garter, but intentionally blocked the view of the photo taker. Another showed her delicately feeding him a sliver of cake, yet another showed him feeding her. In one, she looked up at him, eyes wide and asking for his trust.

That was one battle she'd always fought. He didn't trust easily, not after first his mother, then his fiancée, abandoned him. And now, with the pictures as proof, she saw the underlying tension where her traumatized mind had only remembered happiness.

Pain lanced across her forehead, leaving a pounding in its wake. She needed aspirin, needed...

Her eye was drawn to her wedding ring, and her hand followed. She picked up the plain band as well as her engagement ring and slipped both on her finger.

The thundering in her temples increased, and she momentarily squeezed her eyes shut, desperate to block out the pain.

Shane opened the bathroom door; light glinted off the tiny diamond. She scrambled to her feet, the photo album thudding to the floor. He moved toward her, then stopped and rested his hips against the dresser. His gaze was narrowed, and...

Her heart missed a beat, then another.

And...

In that moment her past crashed back.

She remembered.

Everything.

Every awful, horrible detail, the heartache, the flood of tears, the realization she had no option but to leave him.

Her mouth fell open and her hands dropped helplessly to her sides. Her knees sagged, and she reached to steady herself on the dresser.

"You remember."

"Yes."

"Everything?"

Including the reason she couldn't stay with him. More than ever, she regretted their intimacy, wished she was dressed, rather than facing him in only an oversize shirt. He clearly had the advantage. Freshly showered and shaven, dressed in faded denim and soft cotton, he was all man to her smaller woman.

Quietly he asked, "So you know why you left?"

She nodded, then tipped back her chin to face his fury. She deserved it, she supposed. If the situation were reversed, she would have been furious. "I do."

Whiplash fast, he added, "And you know why the hell you're back?"

"Shane—"

"Why, Angie? Why did you rip my heart out five years ago? And why in God's name are you back? To stomp on it?"

She exhaled a shaky little breath. She refused to be intimidated by Shane, no matter how much a renegade part of her longed to be back in his arms. "I never meant to hurt you," she said honestly.

He scoffed.

In the dull morning light, Shane saw regret in her blue eyes, regret mixed with resolve. This wasn't the woman he'd loved last night, the woman who'd cried out his name.

This was the woman who'd coldly left him.

Part of him wanted to believe their lovemaking had changed something deep inside him, dulling his anger, but it hadn't. Five years of suppressed fury rushed to the surface.

He had a hundred questions—and he vowed to get an answer to each. One question, though, overrode the others. "Where's your dearly beloved husband?"

She shuddered. "I'm not married."

"Two divorces in five years? Not bad for a woman who swore she'd only have one marriage, ever."

"Jack's dead." She sifted a hand through her hair, shifting the locks that had fallen across his chest in sleep. The cut on her forehead stood as a reminder that she wasn't completely recovered, but damn it, she *remembered.*

Her shoulders drooped. "It's been a long time—"

"Five years, four months..." He glanced at the date. "Two days."

She sighed, and her breasts rose, then fell beneath the soft cotton of his shirt. Just the memory of what lay beneath the material had the ability to arouse him, and he coldly shut off his purely reflexive response. Yesterday, last night had been a mistake, one he wouldn't repeat.

"I told myself you would have gotten over me."

He took another step toward her.

"You didn't forget," she said.

"Or forgive."

Even though he'd taken a couple of steps toward her, she stood her ground. The old Angie would have retreated.

"Let's start with now—tell me why the hell you thought it was a good idea to show up, uninvited and unwanted at my house."

She winced. "I was going to my aunt's house."

"Only a fool goes out in a Colorado snowstorm."

"It wasn't snowing at Denver International Airport."

"And it didn't occur to you that we could have a blizzard on this side of the pass? No," he continued, "it wouldn't have. You didn't make it past the second week in September. You never saw a mountain snowstorm, did you?"

"Do you want answers to your questions? Or do you want to rant and rave at me?"

"I don't rant and rave."

"No, you don't," she agreed. "That would have meant exposing part of yourself, showing that you were human."

"What the hell is that supposed to mean?"

"You're always so controlled." She wrapped her arms around her, pulling the shirt up a little higher.

"I don't know about that," he said softly, not having as much success as he'd hoped at ignoring the fact that she was a half-dressed woman, only a few feet from a rumpled, inviting bed.

She dropped her arms. "I'm not talking about sex. That wasn't ever a problem."

"No, it wasn't." His eyes narrowed.

"It was afterward, wasn't it, Shane? Afterward when you'd shut me out?"

"Shut you out? I'd say it was prudent, given the fact you didn't take your vows seriously. Till death do us part—or until Daddy's money shone in your eyes."

"Money meant nothing to me. You knew that."

"Did I?"

"I never wanted gold and diamonds. The only thing I ever wanted was this—" she touched her necklace "—and your belief in me and our love."

"I loved you, Angie."

"I'm going to get dressed." She tipped her chin. "If you want to talk, and if you can do it like a rational adult, we can do it in the living room. Otherwise, I have nothing to say to you."

Neutral ground. But he wouldn't promise to be civilized. The churning in his gut was primitive, not polite. "Your clothes are on the shelf, not in a box."

Breaking eye contact, she turned away.

Her body brushed his as she went into the bathroom. Reacting instinctively, he snagged her wrist, stopping her.

Her eyes flashed, and she pulled her wrist away, going into the bathroom.

When she closed the door, he slammed a fist against his open palm.

He had always been a gentleman before. No woman had ever gotten to him the way she did.

Energy churning in his gut, he left the room and lit a fire, stabbing the wood with a metal poker.

He filled the coffeepot, then walked away from it. He didn't need the jolt of caffeine. Hardhat carried his food dish across the room and dropped it at Shane's feet. Distractedly he filled it, then grabbed his coat and gloves, heading outside to shovel the eighteen inches of heavy, wet snow from the flagstone pathway.

Within ten minutes, Hardhat had pushed open the front door and was barking excitedly as he played, once or twice nearly disappearing as he sunk up to his whiskers in the piles Shane had created.

Shane took off his jacket. He was warm, nearly hot from the exertion. Wasn't complaining, though. As long as he concentrated on what he was doing, he wasn't filled with thoughts of Angie and their rediscovery.

Much.

He shoveled snow from behind his four-wheel drive. Now, as soon as he heard a plow on the main road, he could take Angie back to town.

He wondered why that thought bothered him. He should be glad to see her go.

Shane and Hardhat returned to the quiet house. Hardhat shook snow from his fur, then took up his usual place in front of the fireplace.

"Did you see a snowplow?" Angie asked.

He blinked, trying to clear sunspots from his eyes and focus. She stood near the window, hands wrapped around a steaming cup of coffee. How long had she been there, watching him?

"Not yet. It could be a while."

"I don't suppose you have a snowmobile?"

"Afraid I'll bite?"

He dropped his wet gloves near the coatrack and shoved his fingers through his wet hair. After taking off his boots, he moved toward the fire, standing with his back to it, his arms folded across his chest.

When they'd first married, he'd enjoyed coming home to her at night, tired and sexually hungry. Then, though, she'd met him with a smile and the offer of a back rub.

Now he barely recognized her.

Her long-sleeved button-down shirt was crisply tucked into the waistband of her jeans. Her spine was tight and straight, and her shoulders were pulled back. She'd swept her glorious hair into a no-nonsense twist, and not even a tendril escaped.

While he'd been outside, she'd undergone a transformation, and she wore self-assurance as casually as she did her designer shoes. He could easily imagine her in a boardroom. He had to look deeply for a resemblance between her and the woman who'd trustingly pitched herself into his arms. There was no trace of the shy college graduate who'd come to Colorado to work at her aunt's coffee shop and flex her wings for the summer.

Of course, he wasn't the same man, either.

Five years ago, he'd been distrusting. He'd learned a lot at the hands of his mother, and then his fiancée. Women only stuck around as long as there was something in it for them. When things got rough, they took off.

If he'd been distrustful back then, experience had made him what he was now: hard and cynical, capable of taking what a woman offered physically, then turning his back when they asked for more.

The fireplace sizzled.

"You want answers," she said. "You deserve them." She set her coffee on the windowsill. "I'm not back in town permanently, only for a few weeks. I've got a lot of work to do for my Valentine's Day gala in Chicago. I need to get back to it."

That was a small-enough blessing. But a few weeks was still too many.

"Aunt Emma called me a few months ago to let me know that the town needed a recreation center for kids. She's in Florida right now, so she offered to let me stay in her house. She left the car she sometimes drives—the one you and I bought in Durango—at the airport so I'd have my own transportation."

She started to say something, but then stopped herself, and then added, "I was on my way to her house when I hit a patch of ice and slid into a tree. That's how I ended up at your house."

He had more questions than answers. "What do you have to do with the community center?"

"My organization, Dreams and Wishes, is paying for the new center."

"Your organization? Meaning the one you work for?"

"No, I mean the organization I funded with my own money. When my father died—"

"Your father is dead?"

She took a deep breath, then swallowed. "He and Jack were killed in the same plane accident, two years ago."

This time, Shane did offer his condolences. He despised Edward Burton, but the man was Angie's father. And after the death of her mother when she was young, she'd been very close to her father, even if he was overbearing and overprotective.

God knew, Shane's father had had his share of problems and finally decided that facing a bottle of alcohol was easier than facing life. Despite that, Shane had loved the man. Blood was blood, no matter the faults.

"I was the designated beneficiary on both of their insurance policies, and I inherited the business."

"You run Burton Enterprises, as well?"

"I sold it," she corrected him.

"I tried to tell you." She wrapped her arms around her middle. "I sent you a letter."

He remembered.

Softly she said, "I wanted you to know everything, that I'd loved you. That I hadn't betrayed you."

He'd returned the letter unopened. He and Sarah had gotten on with their lives. Even though it had been three years since Angie had left, he'd decided that he and Sarah didn't need anything from the past interfering with their future. "Your actions spoke loud enough. You proved you weren't different from any other woman. Wasn't interested in your excuses or lies."

She pressed her fingers to her throbbing temple. "I have never lied to you."

"Then why didn't you wait until the ink was dry on our divorce papers to marry Jack?"

"You really believe I wanted to marry him?"

"Looked that way to me, when I showed up at your nuptials, uninvited. He was proposing a toast and you were lifting your glass to him."

"You saw a small portion of my life, and you took it out of context," she said. "I never wanted to be a pawn, never cared about my father's business, or that it would be one of the world's largest computer networking firms if he merged with Jack's company. I was never happier than when I was here in Colorado, working for a living and being responsible for myself.''

''So you used me as a pawn instead. You married me so that you'd have an excuse not to go back to Chicago.''

''You're a fool if you believe that, Shane Masters.'' Her voice shook. ''A hardheaded, stubborn fool. I married you because I fell in love with you.''

He sneered. ''That's why our two month marriage was the shortest in the county's history.''

''Believe what you want.''

''Okay. Assuming I believe you, why did you walk out?''

''To save you.''

''To save me?'' he echoed. ''What are you, some kind of avenging angel? And I'm a man who needs your protection?''

Her blue eyes fired anger as she strode across the room and poked him in the chest.

He caught her wrist and held it.

''Whether you want to believe me or not, everything I did, I did for you.''

She tipped back her head so she could look him square in the eye and said, ''When my father learned of our marriage, he was enraged. He called me at the coffee shop and told me I had twenty-four hours to be back in Chicago. For the first time in my life, I defied him. I told him I was in love, and that I was staying here. Then I hung up on him.''

''You never told me.''

''It didn't matter.''

''Maybe it did.''

Tension hissed and crackled between them. Her self-composure never faltered. In the past, it would have. He realized he didn't know her half as well as he'd thought he did.

She pulled her wrist free of his grip and moved away from him, crossing the room to look out the window for a few seconds.

"That wasn't the end of it." She faced him again. "My dad showed up the next week. It was that morning, after you'd nearly called in sick to work. I was at the coffee shop and my father stormed in. He started yelling at my aunt, calling her irresponsible, telling her he'd trusted her to take care of me, and look what she'd allowed to happen. He should have known better than to believe anything she'd said—after all, she wasn't really family, she was my mother's sister."

Shane softly swore.

"I defended her, told him to leave Emma out of it. Emma hadn't known about my marriage, so there was no way she could have stopped it. Dad said it didn't matter, she'd never get to see me again. She was my godmother, did you know that?

"I guess my mom brought me out to see Auntie Em a few times when I was a child. But Dad was so overprotective after Mom died that he stopped me from going anywhere. Emma said she loved me like the daughter she never had, so when he threatened that she'd never see me again, she cried. I only ever saw her cry twice, once at my mom's funeral, then again that day."

"You took on that guilt."

"Wouldn't you?" she asked quietly. "Then he turned to me, but without anger. He took out a file folder from his briefcase. He'd bought the note on your business loan."

"Hell."

"And on your mortgage. *He owned you, Shane.*"

He furiously drummed his fingers on the bare mantel.

"Everything you'd worked for, everything you'd struggled and fought for, he owned. You didn't know it. He hid behind one of his corporations. He didn't have to be angry with me, because he knew I'd do exactly what he said. He intended to call the note due. He was in control. He had you. And in owning you, he had me."

"I had a right to know."

"I knew you'd see it that way. That's why I couldn't tell you."

"Damn it." He pounded the heel of his palm on the pine mantel. Hardhat looked up and cocked his head. "A partnership, Angie. Wasn't that what you were always insisting on, our marriage being a partnership? Or was that only when it suited you?"

"Would you have let me go?" she asked very quietly.

"Hell, no. You were my wife."

"And that's why I couldn't tell you."

"I would have told your father to shove his threats and thrown him out of the state myself."

"I know. You would have forced me to stay."

"Where you belonged."

"And you wouldn't have given me a choice."

He was being backed into a corner. To him, this was black and white, right and wrong. And she was wrong. "We could have weathered the storm together. Unless you didn't want to."

"And what about Sarah?" Angie extended a hand toward him. "Don't you see? It wasn't just about us. It was about Sarah, too. I would have lived anywhere with you, would have eaten canned beans and noodles for the rest of my life, but it wasn't just about us.

"My dad had a dossier on you. He knew about Sarah, knew she was a minor and that she was living with us.

If he called your loan due, you'd lose everything. His next step was to go to social services. He had connections there. With you having no job, no home, and with his influence, the state would have taken Sarah from you. If I stayed, you would have lost Sarah. You would have been emotionally destroyed, Shane. You would have felt as though you'd failed in your responsibilities to Sarah, and it would have been my fault. I couldn't do that to you. I couldn't force you to choose between your love for me and your love for Sarah.''

"It wasn't your decision to make."

"It was at the time."

"Damn you, Angie, it was my life, my decision."

"And what if I had come to you? What would you have done?'' she challenged. "You couldn't afford a lawyer. Even if you could, there was no way to fight my dad and win. I made the only decision I could for you, for us.''

"Better that I hate you than resent you?" he said, words dripping with bitterness.

"Yes," she whispered. "It's easier."

"So you took the coward's way out and left."

"Put yourself in my position, Shane.''

"I wouldn't have walked out on you."

"I didn't walk out, you hardheaded mule. Saying I walked out implies I had a choice. Because I loved you, I had no choice.

"I'm not your mother. I'm not Delilah. I was a woman who left you because I loved you. Whether you agree or not, it was my decision, and I did the best I could. I wanted you to have a chance at the dreams that drove you. Not that you would have ever appreciated my sacrifice for you and Sarah.'' She shook her head. "I'm not surprised by any of this, that you didn't give me the benefit of the doubt, that you still won't listen to me. Why should you be any different from any other man?''

"I wasn't any other man. I was your husband."

"So I should have let you make the decision and ruin your life, is that it?''

Frustrated, he kissed her, and the depth of his emotion stunned Shane.

Slowly he ended the angry kiss. No woman, ever, had dragged this kind of reaction from him. He'd kept his feelings locked away, and she continually unlocked them. Damn it, if he didn't still care, this wouldn't matter.

"At least that was honest,'' she said, turning away.

Shane told himself that exorcizing the passion was a good thing, that it would help him get over her.

But as she went away, leaving her own special scent lingering behind in the crackling atmosphere, Shane instinctively recognized his own lie.

Having her back in his life hadn't snuffed the emotional flame.

It had only fed it.

Seven

Angie collapsed against the bedroom door, fingers pressed to her mouth and tears flooding her eyes.

She told herself she wouldn't cry. When she left him, she thought she'd cried all the tears she'd ever cry. Now she knew differently.

He hadn't physically hurt her, but emotionally she ached all the way to her soul.

She wished she could turn back time, wished she hadn't stopped beneath that tree, wished she hadn't lost her memory, wished she hadn't made love with him, reminding herself she'd never stopped caring....

A tear escaped and trickled down her cheek.

The weight of the aspen leaf around her neck now felt like an anchor. She'd kept it as a talisman, a reminder of her time with Shane, of the fun times they'd shared. It was as if that part of her wouldn't die, as long as she had a token of the past.

Jack had hated the cheap piece of jewelry and tried to yank it off her neck. But in her first act of defiance, she'd knocked his hand away and told him if he touched it, there wouldn't be a marriage. He'd have to find another pawn to use in the chess game he and her father were playing. Their merger could go to hell and him along with it.

His eyes had narrowed, and he'd backed down, and Angie realized that any hope for a happy future had vanished in that instant. She'd set the rules, and he'd agreed to them. Back then, though, she hadn't realized the emotional cost she'd have to pay or the way he'd use the promise of a child to get her to do what he wanted.

When Jack died and she realized how much he had actually controlled her, she swore she'd live her own life under her own terms. The fight with Shane just now affirmed that she'd made the right choice. She didn't need or want a man, any man.

She had a life, friends and a job she adored. What more could she need?

Her hands shaking, she unfastened the clasp and let the necklace fall into the box near her discarded rings.

Sheriff Spencer McCall pounded on the door. Belatedly Hardhat roused himself and galloped to the door to bark out a warning.

Spencer skipped the greetings. "Found Emma Kelsey's car abandoned down off the county road," he said, shaking snow off his lawman's hat. "And Doc Johnson said he got a call from you about Angie."

"She's here."

Spencer raised a questioning brow.

"Safe and sound." He and Spencer went way back, and Spencer had been there the day Angie left. He and

Slade Birmingham had refused to leave Shane alone. The two men even stayed the night, sleeping on the floor, not believing Shane's promise that he was fine, that an end of a marriage meant nothing, that he wasn't going to do something crazy and hit the bottle like his old man used to.

But Shane had been lying to himself. It mattered, a hell of a lot. After he got back from Chicago, he had bought a bottle of whiskey and toasted his determination to get on with his life.

"Doc said she'd been in an accident, has amnesia."

"Had," Shane corrected him. "She's doing better now."

"And what about you?"

"Never better." The lie tasted bitter.

"Spencer," Angie said, coming out of the bedroom, carrying her purse.

Shane noticed she'd taken off the ring that had glinted on her finger. His stomach clenched.

"It's good to see you," Spencer said to Angie.

Spencer smiled warmly at Angie and extended his hand. She accepted it and gave him a dazzling smile, one Shane knew he'd never see again.

"Are you the sheriff now?" she asked, looking at the star on his jacket.

"Followed in the old man's footsteps," he said, then added, "That was a heck of a hike you took. A couple of miles at least, through a snowstorm."

"I knew Shane would take care of me." For a brief second, she looked at him. Their gazes connected and she quickly looked down. "Of course, if I hadn't had my chimes rung, I might have thought differently."

Tension gusted through the room.

"Doc Johnson's expecting you. Promised I wouldn't come back without you."

"Can you give me a ride to town?"

Shane wondered if that was desperation in her tone.

"Be glad to."

An icicle seemed to stab Shane's spine when she looked at him. She extended her right hand, then let it fall to her side. "Thank you for taking care of me."

She wasn't expressing gratitude as much as saying goodbye.

He nodded tightly but said nothing.

"See you for poker?" Spencer asked Shane.

"Yeah."

Spencer replaced his hat, then took Angie's elbow and guided her to his official sports utility vehicle.

She gave Shane a quick glance over her shoulder before getting in the passenger side.

Shane told himself it was better she leave now rather than later, which she inevitably would. She wasn't planning to be in Colorado long, anyway.

But as Spencer drove off with her, Shane realized that an impersonal goodbye hurt every damn bit as bad as a Dear John letter.

"Around The Town"
by Miss Starr

Miss Starr is delighted to announce that Angela Burton, Emma Kelsey's niece from Chicago, has temporarily returned to town! Rumor had it that Angela was returning to take over her aunt's coffee shop. Your intrepid reporter has learned differently, however. And the truth is much more exciting than anyone could have imagined!

Angela runs Dreams and Wishes, an organization

she established to help meet the needs of youngsters all across the country. While she's here, Angela will be meeting with our very own Reverend Sheffield to discuss plans for the town's community center!

As you know, our children have been using the old school, built in 1904, and the schoolhouse is in desperate need of repair. Dreams and Wishes is riding to the rescue! Reportedly, Emma Kelsey's coffee shop will be used for a temporary community center while repairs are underway.

This is very good news indeed. We owe a huge debt to Miss Emma and her lovely, lovely niece, Angela, whom Miss Starr hopes to see very shortly.

As longtime residents might remember, Angela had a whirlwind marriage with Shane Masters one summer. I have it on very good authority that Angela spent one snowbound weekend at the handsome young man's home.

Valentine's Day is quickly approaching...dare we hope that love is, as well? Stay tuned, as I promise to bring you all the developments as they happen.

For this week, loyal readers, this is all the news you can use.

"This our angel?" a young child asked Reverend Sheffield.

As soon as the child asked the question, she stuck her thumb back into her mouth. Angie guessed the precious girl to be about four, and Matt smiled as he squatted to the child's level.

"Yes, Molly, this is Angela Burton. She's going to be helping us get our new community center." He looked up at her. "Angela, I'd like you to meet Molly Barrett."

Angie crouched alongside Matt. "Hello, Molly, I'm very pleased to meet you."

Molly pulled her thumb from her mouth. "I never met a real-live angel 'fore."

Startling Angie, Molly threw her arms around Angie's neck. Automatically, she hugged the child back.

For a moment, tears threatened to storm her eyes. She'd dreamed of having a child of her own, but had to face the reality that it wasn't going to happen, not now, not ever. That pain hurt every bit as much as the night when, just before his death, Jack had told her that as long as they were married, she would never be a mother. Until then, he'd made promises...telling her that if he could trust her, she could have the family she wanted. Foolishly, she'd believed him...giving up control of her life in small pieces.

But as Molly held on, Angie's heart melted. Working with children had been the right choice for her life, she realized.

When Molly finally let go, Angie said, "I'm not really an angel, you know."

"You're getting us our new com...com..."

"Community center," Matt supplied.

"Right? So as I have somewhere to be when my mommy goes working."

"Well, yes, but—"

"Then you're an angel." She punctuated her sentence by sticking her thumb back in her mouth.

"There's a lot of people around here who feel the same way," Matt told her.

Molly's preschool teacher rushed into the room. "Molly! There you are."

"I's talking to an angel," she said as her teacher took her hand to guide her toward the other children.

"Molly's precious," Angie said softly, her gaze lingering on the direction Molly had taken.

"You're good with her."

"I adore kids."

"It shows."

She met Matt's gaze. She remembered him from the few months she'd lived here. Back then, he hadn't been a man of the cloth; he'd been a rowdy young man, undecided whether to finish college or go to auto mechanics school. Life had taken them both different directions. "Do you like being a minister?" she asked suddenly.

"Can't think of anything I'd rather do. What about you, Angie, are you satisfied with your life? You and Shane once talked about having kids of your own."

"I'm happy," she said, ignoring the little wrench in her heart. "I love what I do with the kids. I'd like to think I make a difference."

"You do," he said.

When he started to ask another question, she changed the subject, asking about the building's current plumbing and what they'd have to do to bring it up to code.

After completing the tour, she and Matt returned to his office in the church and went over the architect's plans.

"These are good," she approved after studying the blueprints. "I like that she proposes to keep it as original as possible, but updating the plumbing and adding new windows. I like that we can have alcoves for the kids so it's quieter at nap times. I also like the separate areas for the preschool and day-care sections." She flipped a page. "This gymnasium will be wonderful. Does the town have a gymnastics team?"

"Not right now." He leaned back in his chair. "We don't have the equipment. Kids who are interested have to go to Fairplay."

"That makes it tough," she sympathized. "How about volleyball and basketball?"

"Just at the high school."

"So this could really benefit the younger kids." She grinned. Blood was singing in her veins. This was what she loved, making a difference. "Do you have a contractor in mind?"

"I do."

She looked up, frowning when he didn't immediately answer.

"Masters Construction."

She sucked in a small breath. "Shane's company."

"They're the best we have locally."

"What about contractors in Durango or Denver?"

"This is your project, Angela. You can hire whoever you want."

"But—"

"Shane does a great job, has his own crew instead of hiring subcontractors, stands behind his work and he's reasonably priced. He did the work on the church when we remodeled two years ago. I can personally vouch for him. And you saw what he did with his house."

A flush rushed up her cheeks. Did the whole town know she'd spent a few days with her ex-husband? She never had this problem in Chicago. Then again, in the big, anonymous city, few people cared.

"I take it you haven't seen the *Courier?*"

"The *Courier?*"

"Once a week the newspaper runs a gossip column, written anonymously by Miss Starr. She reported you'd weathered the storm at Shane's place. Even if she hadn't,

I heard about it from Doc Johnson. He figured a few extra prayers for your safety couldn't hurt.''

Her legs no longer able to support her, Angie sat down across from Matt.

"You okay?" he asked.

"Is that the town's minister asking?"

"An old friend," he corrected her. "Unless you need a minister to talk to, in which case, I'm all ears."

She shook her head. "I'm fine."

"Have you been sleeping?"

"Not a lot," she confessed with a wan smile.

"Doc says there're few remnants of the injury. Does that mean there's something else on your mind?"

Matthew Sheffield had the kindest eyes she'd ever seen. Blue, nearly gray, they spoke of compassion. Even though his words were probing, his tone was gentle, holding no nosiness. If she didn't want him to push, he wouldn't. "I had amnesia," she said. "I didn't remember that Shane and I had divorced."

"I understand."

She thought that maybe he did. After closing her eyes for a moment, trying to shut out the exhaustion of four nights of broken sleep and haunted dreams, she looked at Matt and honestly said, "He'll never see that I did the only thing I could."

"I take it you explained things to him?"

"Tried," she said sadly. "He sees life in black and white."

"Most of us do, Angela."

"Angie," she said. "I became Angie again when Jack died."

"Angie, then," he agreed. "We're all human, we all have failings, we all make mistakes. The trick is to pick up the pieces and go on, try to make the world a better place from where we are, not where we were.''

''I'm trying, Matt. I'm trying.''

''And so is Shane. He's doing the best he can.''

She instinctively reached for the aspen leaf, only to realize it wasn't there. She dropped her hand to her lap and curled it into an empty fist. ''I just wish I'd never had to hurt him.''

''And that's why you're doing this for the town? To make up for the hurt?''

''Superman's not the only one with X-ray vision, apparently.''

He grinned. ''Was I talking like a minister?''

''No,'' she said. ''You were being a friend. I appreciate it.''

Matt took a phone call, and for the first time, she began to question the choices she'd made in her life. Molly's hug and Matt's concern brought up questions Angie was trying hard not to face.

After he ended the call, Matt brought the conversation back around to Shane's company. ''The decision of who to hire is strictly yours. I won't try and influence you.'' He steepled his hands on top of the desk.

''I need to think about it.''

''I know you'll reach the right decision.''

''You have more faith in me than most people.''

Matt grinned. ''That's my job.''

After a few minutes of discussion, she stood. ''When I've hired a contractor, I'll be in touch.''

''Thanks, Angel. Maybe that name'll stick.''

With a small smile, she waved goodbye.

Outside, she buttoned her coat against the bite of cold air sweeping down from Eagle's Peak. The entire mountain was still white from the storm. Even though they'd had a lot of sunshine, the temperatures had prevented the snow from melting. The landscape looked as bleak as her heart suddenly felt.

She walked toward the Chuckwagon Diner, needing a cup of coffee to warm up and to think. Shane probably was a good choice for the job but she couldn't work with him, not after their argument and lovemaking.

She arrived at the Chuckwagon just as huge flakes of snow began to fall from a nearly clear blue sky.

"Come in, come in," Bridget Potter greeted. The older woman waved her onto a stool near the ancient bar. "My goodness gracious, child, it's been about five years since we've seen you around here. Your aunt Emma told me you'd be stopping by."

"It's good to be back, Bridget." Angie realized she truly meant it.

Until now, she hadn't realized how much she'd missed this little town. When she went back to Illinois, she'd tried to cut out her memories of Colorado, pretend that part of her life had never happened. It had only been a summer, she'd rationalized.

But it had been so much more.

She'd formed relationships here, and she was welcomed back as if she were family. Sitting here under Bridget's watchful eye and with a cup of hot, steaming coffee placed in front of her without her having to ask, Angie realized just how much she'd lost in leaving. It wasn't just Shane, it was a way of life.

"Aren't you supposed to be resting like Doc Johnson said?"

"I'm doing much better." Besides, resting only gave her mind time to remember Shane...the way his eyes darkened with desire and the fury that burned them when he saw that she remembered intentionally hurting him.

The sooner she got started with her meetings, the sooner she'd be on her way, with Shane just a part of her past once more.

"I saw your Shane this morning."

"He's not my Shane," she said softly, sipping from the coffee and looking at Bridget through the steam.

"Go on with you, now. You spent last weekend together."

"Does everyone know?"

"Everyone with eyes or ears. If you don't be reading Miss Starr's column yourself, you'll hear about it soon enough."

She sighed. "He took care of me, Bridget. Nothing more."

"If'n you say so, missy." She turned to flip a burger on the grill behind her. "What can I get for you?"

"How about a piece of pie? Do you still make pecan yourself?"

"I do indeed." She looked at Angie purposefully. "But you need something more substantial than pie. What with trying to recover from that nasty car accident." She tutted.

Family? Angie wondered. No, the caring of the people here went deeper than that. Her mother had loved Angie deeply, but after Sylvia died, when Angie was a young teen, no one ever asked if she'd eaten. Her father figured she was eating at school—either that or the housekeeper had fed her.

Until this moment, she hadn't realized how much she'd lost and how much she cherished being part of a family, extended or not.

"You still enjoy a nice bacon, lettuce and tomato sandwich?"

"Haven't had one in five years."

The woman harrumphed, then said, "Well, I'll be taking care of that problem right away, then."

Angie took another sip of coffee while Bridget tossed some bacon on the sizzling grill.

"You know, your Shane doesn't look any better than you do."

She didn't want to be interested. So why did her heart run its next five beats into one? "Oh?"

"He looks tired, as if he hasn't slept. Bernadette Simpson from the post office made sure he knew you went to Doc Johnson and that the doc gave you a clean bill of health."

"Bridget! I'm sure it didn't matter to him one way or another."

"Then you'd be thinking wrong."

"I doubt it."

"He asked about you."

Her heart rushed its next two beats together. "He did?"

"Indeedy."

"Just in passing, I'm sure," Angie said. "We both have separate lives. And I'm anxious to get back to Chicago and my work there."

"And when might that be?"

"In a few weeks." Then, suspiciously, she narrowed her eyes. "You wouldn't be Miss Starr, would you?"

"Me?" Bridget laughed, then served up the hamburger and called for the waitress. "Heavens to Betsy, missy. When would I have time to be a gossip columnist? I'm here seven days a week as it is."

"You seem to know everything in town. I'll bet most people stop by eventually."

"Still and all, I'm not Miss Starr."

A few minutes later, Bridget returned to refill Angie's

coffee cup. ''I need some advice,'' Angie told the woman.

''Now, that's something I can be giving. No extra charge.''

''I'm looking for a contractor for the community center.''

''You'll be hiring Shane, without a doubt.''

She swallowed her groan. ''I was hoping there were other contractors in town.''

''There certainly are.'' She liberally spread a layer of mayonnaise on Angie's toast.

Angie didn't usually eat anything that wasn't healthy, but now she was salivating. Yes, there was definitely something wonderful about being back in Colorado.

''I hired Sammy Dawson one time because Shane was busy and I needed an emergency repair on my front steps. They're wooden, you know, and one of 'em collapsed when Bea Hampton was on them.''

''Bea Hampton?'' She remembered the elderly matron, the town's unofficial first lady. ''Was she hurt?''

''No, just her pride.'' Bridget smiled conspiratorially. ''But she broke a heel off one of her Rodeo Drive shoes.''

''She must have been indignant.''

''Furious. Sent me a bill for a new pair of shoes. Lordy, Lordy, but I had to sell a lot of hamburgers to pay that bill.''

Angie shook her head.

''Well, anyway, Sammy had made such a mess of the repairs that the whole set came down the same day he fixed 'em.'' Bridget brandished a spatula. ''Our Shane had to come and save me. Did a mighty fine job, as well, he did.''

She didn't doubt it. She had seen his handiwork at the

house, and there was no doubt as to the quality or his eye for detail. But that didn't mean she wanted to work side by side with her ex-husband. "Do you know of any Denver firms who might be able to do the job?"

"In winter?" She propped her hands on her hips. "Missy, are you plannin' to get this project of yours started before spring?"

She slid the delicious-looking sandwich and a pile of hot fries in front of Angie, then started work on the next order.

After enjoying the meal and a piece of pecan pie "on the house" and thanking Bridget, Angie returned to her car, passing Shane's office on the way.

She didn't stop, didn't even peek in the window. She and Shane were in the past, and maybe their marriage shouldn't have ever happened, anyway. Still, even after telling herself he didn't matter to her, she wondered if he was as tired as Bridget said he was.

By the time Angie drove to her aunt's Victorian, the sun had been swallowed by Eagle's Peak. Snow drifted downward in huge flakes and clouds blocked the moon and stars. There were no sounds, and no one was out. For all she knew she could have been alone in the world.

She grabbed the blueprints and a pile of mail from the back seat of the car and trudged through the snow, then went inside the cold, dark house. Funny, it had never seemed this big or lonely before.

After lighting a fire and turning on the teakettle, she picked up the pile of mail and found the newspaper. She turned to Miss Starr's column and read it, word for word.

When she reached the end, she sank into a high-back chair at the table, the newspaper falling to the side. Miss Starr wrote that Valentine's Day was quickly approaching and wondered if love could be far behind. It could be, Angie knew, very, very far behind. She might have spent the weekend with him, but Shane had simply been fulfilling a duty. He'd have done the same for anyone.

A renegade part of her reminded her of the lovemaking. It had been incredible, she mentally conceded, but it didn't mean anything to him. They were both adults, they'd both felt the flare of desire and they'd acted on it. People in confined places often behaved that way. It meant nothing.

Why, then, did her heart ache?

With determination, she threw herself into her work, seeking—and finding—solace there.

She read her e-mail, then called her office, checked on the details for the huge Valentine's fund-raiser for Dreams and Wishes, asked her assistant to "overnight" the latest financial reports and confirmed the date she'd be back in Chicago.

Talking to Judy, Angie was in her element. When she hung up, she felt fulfilled and renewed, like she had during her meeting with Matt.

She had her work. That was all she needed, all she wanted.

The kettle shrilled and she turned off the burner, forgetting about brewing a pot of tea as she pored over the community center blueprints. It was an exciting project, a renovation the town desperately needed. Tomorrow, she'd find a contractor—someone other than her ex-husband—and get the bid process started.

That decision turned out to be easier said than done.

She spent the entire next morning on the telephone to Denver construction firms and found only one willing to place a bid. She had no better luck with firms in Durango or Breckenridge.

When the preliminary Denver bid was faxed over at

noon, she shook her head in frustration. The rate was exorbitant and they wouldn't be able to get a crew out for at least a month. If she hired them, she'd be over-budget and past her hoped-for deadline.

Angie was well and truly stuck.

Telling herself that she could be professional for the kids' sake, that she could put aside her personal feelings for Shane, she dressed conservatively, even pinning up her hair, then packed up the blueprints and drove into town.

Her heart was thudding when she navigated through the snow and into a parking spot near his building. She squared her shoulders and headed for his office.

Courage and determination crumbled when she saw him.

He was standing with his back to her, a phone propped between his shoulder and ear, studying blueprints as he talked. He'd obviously had his hair cut, but it was still long enough that she itched to run her fingers through it. A flannel shirt was stretched across his broad shoulders. His jeans were tight and denim hugged his hips and muscular thighs.

She suddenly remembered being in his arms....

Feeling like a coward, she knew she couldn't do this. Mouth dry, she decided to leave before he saw her.

And then it was too late.

Eight

Turning, Shane saw her.

He crossed the room in a half-dozen steps and snagged her wrist, forgetting the five-year chasm. He stopped her from leaving, something he hadn't been able to do when it really mattered. "What can I do for you?"

"I...er..."

Had it really only been less than a week since he'd seen her? It seemed like yesterday. It seemed like years.

Shane hadn't wanted her leaving to matter to him, but it had. Everywhere he went in his home, he remembered her. He recalled the way she hummed when she was in the kitchen, the way her hair spread across his pillow, the way she curled beneath a Navajo blanket in front of the fire, the scent of her after a shower, the feel of her body pressed against his as she sought his warmth in sleep.

She'd only been at his house a few days, but she'd

insinuated herself back into his life, the very place he didn't want her. It had taken him years to forget her, but the lessons would linger forever.

Despite his resolve, he'd worried about her, wondering if she saw Dr. Johnson, wondering if she'd received a clean bill of health.

When he'd stopped in at the post office, the postmistress, Bernadette, had said Angie had been in to pick up the mail. She looked fine, Bernadette had said, not that he'd asked.

She licked her lower lip and he dropped her wrist, feeling as though he'd been punched in the gut. Just the sight of the tip of her tongue, moist and pink, made him ravenous.

After she left, he'd thrown himself back into his business, working sixteen-hour days. Must have been exhaustion that was torturing him now.

"I have blueprints," she said.

"For?"

"The new community center."

He nodded, trying to focus on her words, not her mouth. "The town's excited about the project. Matt stopped by yesterday and said you'd been out to tour the site yourself. You even made Miss Starr's column."

"You saw it."

"Don't worry, I won't kiss you or rip your clothes off while we're in plain view of the street."

"I wasn't worried about that," she said primly.

"I figured we'd do it in the back room."

She flushed and her hand tightened on the blueprints. He didn't know what made him say that. He'd planned to avoid her completely, not taunt her, and himself, with thoughts of their lovemaking.

"I'm here to see you on business."

She tucked an errant strand of hair behind her ear. The wayward wisp had escaped from the unappealing knot of hair fastened with a plain black band.

That, combined with the light makeup, stiffly ironed blouse, woolen blazer fastened with a big brass button and slim-fitting skirt, was chosen to make her look professional and aloof rather than attractive. In order not to see through the disguise to the beautiful woman beneath, he'd have to be blind. And Shane Masters had perfect vision.

Even dressed like this, with a hands-off warning flashing in the blue of her eyes, he remembered her smiles, her laugh and the way she seemed to care. She tempted him.

"Are you interested in discussing business, Shane?"

He folded his arms and propped his hips against a drafting table. "What have you got in mind?"

"I'd like you to bid on the community center job."

"You want me to work for you?"

"I don't have any other options."

"You tried."

"Denver, Durango and Breckenridge," she said.

She squared her shoulders, like the businesswoman she wanted to be. Underneath, though, he knew her skin was silky and soft, her responses feminine and honest. Why did he want that exposed?

"I only found one firm in Denver that was interested in submitting a bid."

"And I'm your last resort?"

"I understand you do great work."

"Glad you checked my references."

She squirmed. The rolled blueprints bent in half beneath the pressure she exerted. "Shane, don't..."

"Don't what?" he asked silkily. "Don't be honest?

Don't pretend you're my ex-wife? Don't pretend that I can see you'd still rather be anywhere else but in my office, my life, my bed?''

She paled.

"Is that it, Angie? You want to waltz in here, hoping I'll forget the past happened?'' He unfolded his arms and curled his hands into fists at his sides. "Let's be mature businesspeople coming together for the good of the town. It's not supposed to matter that you tried three towns and dozens of contractors, even asking around town for any other option before coming to me, is it?

"Is it, Angie?''

She tipped her chin. "I was hoping...''

"What?''

"Like you said, that we could be mature businesspeople, coming together for the good of the town. I thought that's what you'd want.''

He shook his head. In four strides, he'd devoured the distance between them. "I want your honesty, for once. No acts, no pretensions.'' Reaching behind her, he tugged the band from her hair, freeing the silky strands and watching them float around her shoulders. He grabbed her shoulders, holding her tightly. Something tangible swept over him, and she must have felt it, too, because she shivered. "I want *you* to tell me what you want.''

"This is what I want,'' she protested.

"Tell me,'' he insisted, backing off a step before he gave into the impulse of burying his hands in her hair.

She'd always had this effect on him, from the second he'd seen her five years ago at the coffee shop to the moment she'd pitched herself in his arms a week ago. No other woman made him lose control, no other woman made him feel this raw.

"I came here as a businesswoman, not as Angie. I want you to work up a bid, to help me on this project."

"So tell me about Angie."

"I'll admit it, I came to you last, out of desperation." Beneath her death grip, the blueprints were bent in half, but he saw the change in her, from the woman who'd walked in, to the woman he knew she was.

"I wish there was someone else. I'd rather work with another company, anyone else, someone who doesn't..." She took a breath and he waited.

When she spoke again, she backtracked. "Someone I haven't made love with, someone who doesn't know my darkest secrets." She blinked, admitting, "Someone who doesn't hate me."

"I don't hate you, Angie," he said softly, recognizing the truth and not knowing how he felt about that. Might be easier if he did hate her.

"You don't trust me."

"Don't trust any woman," he corrected her. "I don't need to trust you."

"So, we can work together?"

The sane part of him told him to send her away. The more primal part that had never been able to deny her anything responded, "Show me the blueprints."

She did and he was amazed by her contagious enthusiasm. He'd never intended to refuse to help her, but he hadn't planned to see the renovation as anything more than another project. He was getting caught up in her plans and didn't want to stop it. Maybe he'd have been better off dealing with the aloof businesswoman rather than the softer, more accessible Angie.

"Why don't we go to the schoolhouse," she suggested finally, "so I can show you exactly what I want."

He nodded, then turned on the answering machine and grabbed a jacket.

"How about a bell?" she asked as they walked side by side down the wooden boardwalk. "We could add a big bell at the top of the roof, like they used to have on the old schoolhouses. The building would be renovated to look more like an old-fashioned school, instead of a brand-new community center that might look out of place. We could undo the building's 'modern' facade that the town added in the 1960s. What do you think?"

"Since it's so near the church, I like it."

Inside, she gave him the grand tour, stopping in the office Matt Sheffield and the center's director shared. "She's got a great plan," Matt said. "Don't you agree?"

"Yeah. I do." Strangely it didn't pain him to admit it.

"Are you going to do the work?" Matt asked.

"He is, if I can talk him into it," Angie said. "We need his talent."

After setting up a meeting with Angie for the next day, Matt excused himself, saying he needed to get back to the church.

"What's Matt's involvement?" Shane asked as she led him to the small office she'd staked out as her own.

"The church gives a lot of money to the current center, a community service type of thing. Matt feels strongly that all children should have someplace to go that they feel welcome, regardless of their income. I agree with him.

"Matt knows the town, knows its needs, so I want to work closely with him to make sure we get this community what it needs."

The room she was using as an office was sparsely

decorated. There was a table with files neatly stacked on the right side, a pencil holder on the left and a laptop computer in the middle. She'd also added a handful of blooming plants. Professional and feminine, the room suited her to a T, and he began to see her as more than just the woman who'd left him.

Within minutes, she'd taken off her blazer and draped it across a chair. She moved around the room, punctuating the air with her excited hand movements. Her hair floated freely around her shoulders, and she smiled. "So," she asked breathlessly, "will you submit a bid?"

"Are you this energetic with your fund-raising efforts?"

"Better," she said. "People like to open their checkbooks at my galas."

"Remind me to stay home." His attempted humor fell flat and served as a reminder that he'd always be at his home while she was at hers. "I'll send you a bid," he said. "In the next few days."

She nodded, and he noted her excitement had slipped a notch. "Matt'll be pleased." She curved her hands around the back of a chair and quietly said, "I haven't told you, and I should have, but I admire your work."

"I've learned a lot over the years."

"Even back then, I believed in you. I knew you were going to be the best."

And that was one of the reasons she'd left, or so she'd said, so that he'd have the chance to develop his business.

He nodded and left, but her words haunted him the rest of the day. It wasn't just her words, he realized, it was the way her light perfume lingered in his office—her innocent touch lingered on his arm. He couldn't concentrate on the blueprints in front of him, or on the billing he was doing because his secretary was out with a cold.

As he shuffled through papers and thought about his empty cabin, he told himself he was better off without a woman who ran away from problems.

Why, then, couldn't he get Angie's smile out of his mind? ·

Working with Shane was going to be a piece of cake.

That morning, Angie had actually convinced herself of the fact. Now she laughed at the ridiculous thought. Her businesslike demeanor had lasted right up until the moment he'd pulled the band from her hair.

She sank into the chair behind her desk and stared at the blinking cursor on the laptop's screen. Up until this point she'd managed to keep moving through the day. It was easier when there were a lot of people around and she had phones to answer and concerns to deal with. But now the old schoolhouse was empty and her thoughts had time to catch up to her.

No one, not even Jack, had ever been able to see through the image she presented to the world. Shane saw through it—her—in less than a second.

Shane not only saw through her, he let her know it. He'd pulled the band from her hair, held her around the shoulders, and for a minute, time had fallen away. She'd wanted to touch him, give into the spark that raged, no matter how she tried to douse it.

What was it about him? What was it about her when she was with him...?

Shane spelled danger.

The sooner they got this job done, the better.

That thought spurring her into action, she went home

and changed into blue jeans, tennis shoes and an old T-shirt, then turned around and headed back into town.

As she drove down Front Street, she noticed the light was still on in Shane's office and his four-wheel-drive vehicle was parked out front, the windshield iced over. She wondered if he was going home, if he was going to eat dinner, then decided it was none of her business. She told herself she'd wonder the same about anyone. She was just feeling neighborly concern.

Her hurting heart knew otherwise.

Entering the schoolhouse, she flooded a few rooms with light, banishing the shadows, then called out for a pizza before going into a storage closet for paint supplies.

After dragging a ladder into a corner of an empty room, she slid in a Shania Twain CD, set it to "Any Man of Mine" and cranked up the volume. Then she climbed the ladder and began singing along to the music. She was reaching over her head, painting the ceiling with broad, long strokes, when she heard a shout. "What the hell do you think you're doing?"

Startled, she jumped, nearly losing her balance. Shane was there, grabbing her and lowering her to the wooden floor. Their bodies were pressed against each other's, and a flood of longing gripped her womb.

Sensuality arced through her, pulsing in the room along with the music.

She wanted him with the same intensity she'd wanted him while they were snowbound.

Intentionally she blocked out the feeling. She was no longer a vulnerable woman, and she wouldn't act as if she were. Stiffening her spine, she pulled away from him.

White paint had splashed on his navy cotton shirt, but

he didn't seem to notice. His green eyes flashed fury and his fingers bit into her upper arms. "What the hell are you doing?" he demanded again, shouting to be heard.

"Painting."

"You're not supposed to be on a ladder."

"Doc Johnson gave me a clean bill of health," she insisted, wondering why she was even trying to explain herself to this infuriating man.

"He told you to avoid strenuous activities."

"You asked?"

"I heard," he corrected her.

"My life is none of your business."

His eyes narrowed and heated fury cooled into green granite.

"Let me go," she said.

He did, and suddenly she missed his touch.

Pretending her hand wasn't shaking, she laid the paintbrush across the can and turned off the music. "Did you want something?"

He dragged a hand through his hair, making the grooves next to his eyes even more visible. From the short time they'd been together, she still recognized the layer of tension on his face. He'd obviously been working too many hours, sleeping too few. She nearly gave in to the impulse of rubbing her fingers across his neck and shoulders like she might have, once upon a time.

"I wanted to double-check a few details for the bid. Called your house. When there wasn't an answer, I figured you'd still be here. You've always worked too hard."

"And so have you," she countered.

"I didn't come here for an argument." He held up a hand in truce. "I came to ask about the time frame."

"The time frame?"

"For completing the renovations."

She let out a breath. It was so easy to stiffen her spine for an argument. Maybe she was prickly, she realized. But she'd struggled too hard for her independence to let any man tell her what to do. "I'd like the job finished before tourist season. I could even arrange a bonus if it were completed early.

"Aunt Emma's letting the kids use the coffee shop for now, and the senior center is offering some space, as well. But Auntie Em will need us to be out of there when the tourists arrive."

"I thought you'd only be here a few weeks."

"You're right. I'll probably have to fly back and forth a couple of times. But I'm expected to be home about a week before the Valentine's Day Gala. It's my yearly fund-raiser."

"Where wallets become lighter."

"I'll do nearly anything to part people from their money, if it's for a good cause." She laughed, and so did he. For a second, it was as if the past hadn't happened. Her laughter faded.

She expected him to leave. Instead, he rolled up his shirtsleeves. "What are you doing?"

"Helping you."

"Helping me?"

"If I'm going to be the contractor, there's a lot of work to be done."

"You haven't submitted a bid."

He stopped, mid-roll, and glanced up at her.

There was something so incredibly sexy about rolled-back sleeves and exposed forearms. Why hadn't she seen that before?

"Are you turning down free help?" he asked.

The businesswoman in her knew she shouldn't be so

stubborn. At home, she'd often call her friends and offer pizza and soda to anyone who'd show up. But instinct urged her to send him away. This wasn't a big room. They'd definitely be bumping into each other. It was night and intimate, and she was very much aware of him.

What was best for the center conflicted with what was best for her.

"Let me put it this way, Angie. I'm not letting you go back up that ladder."

"Shane..."

"Don't let your pride stand in the way, Ang. You shouldn't be exerting yourself. The doctor said so."

His voice changed, dropping an octave until it was cajoling and seductive. "You'll get through the work twice as fast with my help."

But that wasn't the point. The point was to kill time, so she wasn't home alone with thoughts of him. *Being* with him would only be worse.

"Accept my help, Angie."

Was she losing her mind? "This isn't on the clock?"

He shook his head. "You should take advantage of me. I don't give a lot of freebies."

"Do you always win?"

"Yeah." He smiled, a disarming grin that melted the rest of her resistance.

"I'll do the ceilings," he said. "You do the lower half of the walls."

She *had* lost her mind.

Angie turned the music back on and restarted the song. Then she grabbed a paintbrush for Shane and offered it to him.

"Did you pick this CD on purpose?"

"I like it."

He took the brush and fanned the bristles. "And the song?"

"It's my favorite."

"Any man of yours better walk the line?"

"Someone has to, and it isn't going to be me."

"You're getting sassy."

"I'm learning."

Shane climbed the ladder, and she dropped to her knees to work on the baseboard. A drop of paint splattered on her head.

"Sorry."

"You don't sound sorry," she said suspiciously. "Are you feeling sassy yourself?"

"Men aren't sassy."

"Sure," she said, wiping the paint from her forehead.

In a short amount of time, the room was finished.

Working so close to him played havoc with her resolve to see him as nothing other than a contractor. Each time she glanced up, she saw his slim hips and muscular thighs. She couldn't help but notice the way his Wranglers conformed to his behind....

She put down her brush and said, "How about a soda?"

"How about a beer?"

"This is a kids' center."

"Soda sounds fine."

"Thought it might." She escaped. Until she was in the tiny kitchenette, she hadn't realized how fast her heart was pounding or how hot she'd become.

She'd sworn off men, all men, so it wasn't possible for any man to have this overwhelming effect on her, especially her ex-husband.

"Thought I'd come and get it."

Startled, she felt her pulse stutter. She turned to face

him, then backed up a step when she saw how close he stood. Only inches from her, he filled the doorway, and his purely masculine scent flooded the atmosphere.

She handed him a soda, then sat at the tiny table.

He joined her, taking a long, deep drink from the soda. They'd shared a lot at the cabin, but that time had been unreal. She'd thought herself to be in love with him and was focused on little else but the enforced—and wanted—emotional intimacy.

Now she saw him as a man who gave his all to whatever he was involved with, whether it was getting together a bid, even volunteer work. On a whole new level, he attracted her. And that made her doubly wary.

He reached over, capturing a lock of hair between his fingers. She ran her tongue over her teeth and studied the bead of sweat running down the aluminum can.

"You've got more paint on your hair than on the wall."

"That's partially your fault."

He rubbed at the paint, then brushed it from her hair. The act would have been natural between lovers. As it was, she could barely breathe.

Wondering what he was doing, Shane released the strand of hair and dropped his hand. He'd stopped by to clear up a few things on the bid, not to get involved with her on a personal level.

He hadn't needed to help her paint, but there was something about her he couldn't resist. And damn it, she needed someone to make sure she followed doctor's orders.

Someone pounded on the door and Shane went to answer it, returning with a gooey veggie supreme pizza. "Dinner?"

"Enough to share. If you're hungry?"

"Yeah." He was, but wondered if staying was smart. Then he thought of his home, lonely and with an empty refrigerator. He slid the pizza on the small table and sat next to her. "Thanks."

She took a bite and melted cheese dripped onto her chin. She laughed and he reached over to swipe it away. Instead he kissed her.

It wasn't planned, wasn't welcome, but there it was, hot and searing, making him want.

When she pulled away, he saw her drag in a few deep breaths, saw her pulse pounding in her throat. His was doing the same.

"Thanks for your help," she said, standing so quickly she nearly knocked over a chair.

"Sure."

After she put away the leftovers, she joined Shane in the other room. Together they finished painting, then cleaned the brushes, saying nothing about the kiss. Then surveyed their handiwork.

"We did a good job," she said.

"Yeah." At one time, he'd thought they would make a good team.

"Let me know when the bid's ready."

After agreeing, Shane shrugged into his jacket and headed outside. He welcomed the cold, better than the sizzling heat that had burned between him and Angie. He should be able to keep his hands to himself. But when she was around, it was impossible.

Her car was dusted with snow and the windows were crusted with an eighth-inch of frost. Without stopping to think, he grabbed his ice scraper and cleaned off her car.

Without a doubt, she was independent enough to scrape her own windows. She might not even appreciate his efforts, even though the old Angie would have been touched.

But this confident woman was no longer the same young woman who'd arrived in town for the summer, having just graduated from college with a business degree in her mind and dreams of being a success in her heart.

She was no longer as vulnerable. She'd grown and changed. She was the success she'd imagined, taking her vision and combining it with knowledge and determination. According to Matt, Dreams and Wishes was one of the best-funded charitable organizations in the country.

She'd established it with her own money and was relentless in fund-raising activities. She gave college and camp scholarships, anything, really, as long as it had to do with kids. He knew she'd wanted her own children. So why didn't she have any?

He couldn't help being intrigued.

Driving home, he wondered why he tortured himself with thoughts of her. If she wanted them to be business associates, then business associates were what they'd be.

Sure an inner voice taunted.

At home, Hardhat barked excitedly and dashed over, then trotted back to the fireplace and looked at Shane expectantly. After lighting a fire, more for the dog than himself, Shane tried not to think of the things he'd missed by keeping women at a distance—companionship, sex, love, being abandoned...

He'd had enough of the last for a lifetime. If he protected himself from facing loss again, he would willingly go without the others.

That decision had been easier earlier in the week, before he'd spent the evening with Angie working together, laughing together, eating together, like they used to, another lifetime ago.

Shane raked a hand through his hair.

When she'd stayed with him, he'd thought that sleeping with her would extinguish the flame, but it hadn't. It had only fed it. Which left him with a hell of a problem. He desired a woman he could never have, a woman he would never trust. He didn't know what to do about it, but only one thing was sure: His protective armor was starting to crack and that meant working with Angie would only get more difficult....

Nine

"**W**ell?" Shane asked, pushing back his chair from the desk and standing to greet her.

"We have a deal," she said. Her throat suddenly dried, so she swallowed deeply. Even though she hadn't seen him over the weekend, she'd thought of him constantly, remembering the hardness of his kiss and the reactive softening inside her.

She didn't welcome her response to him. She didn't want to be involved with any man, but no man, ever, had had the effect on her that Shane did.

Walking in here today was as difficult as she'd imagined it would be, and she'd stalled over a third cup of coffee at the Chuckwagon Diner. She'd chatted with Matt, Bridget and Bernadette and answered Bernadette's endless questions.

It surprised Angie that Shane didn't already know she was coming to see him. "As soon as you sign the contract," she told him, "I'll have a check overnighted to you."

"Deal."

He offered his hand and she reluctantly accepted. The instant hers was engulfed in his firm grip, she was reminded this was anything but business as usual. Men she dealt with didn't make her insides tighten, didn't make her lose track of her next thought. It wasn't until he released her that she could talk at all. "When can you start?"

"Next week."

"I'll be leaving soon." She worried her lower lip and glanced at him. "I was hoping you could start tomorrow."

"Tomorrow?" He arched a brow.

"Unless you're free this afternoon."

"You don't want much, do you?"

"The foundation's good for the money."

"Wasn't worried about that."

"Then...?"

"I have other projects scheduled."

"As important as this?" she asked. "This is for the kids. They deserve a wonderful place to play and create. They're going to be cramped at the coffee shop and senior center. In fact, Matt has had to open some of the classrooms at the church to accommodate the overflow. What could be more important than getting this project—for the whole town—started?"

"You're a shrewd woman, Angie."

"So you'll arrange it?"

"Maybe I can hire an extra couple of guys."

"Yes! Yes, yes, yes, yes, ye-es!" She curled her hand into a victorious fist. "I knew I could count on you." She'd won, the kids had won. "Thank you, Shane.

Matt'll appreciate it, my aunt will appreciate it, the kids will appreciate it. *I* appreciate it.''

He hooked a thumb in a denim belt loop. "Do you?"

In response, she excitedly hugged him, then instantly regretted her enthusiasm. He remained stiff and she quickly moved away.

What was wrong with her? Last night had proved he was the last man she should hug.

He took his seat. "I'll try to rearrange my crew's schedule," he said, unbending a paper clip, then scrunching it up.

"So I'll see you today?"

He glanced up. "You'll see a crew tomorrow," he corrected her. "If I can rearrange their schedules."

Which was much better than she'd dared hope for; after all, his bid didn't say he'd begin work before February 1. "You won't be there yourself?"

He dropped the paper clip in the wastebasket. "I'll periodically oversee the project."

"What about the quality?"

"I personally guarantee my crews' work."

"I see." Telling herself it was best if they didn't deal with each other, even if the knowledge was like a knot in her stomach, she thanked him and left.

At the end of the day, she drove home, hungry and tired. She'd spent part of the day on the telephone to her assistant, the rest helping Matt and other volunteers moving tables, chairs, arts and crafts supplies and all the equipment from the gymnasium over to the coffee shop, senior center and the church. Her muscles ached and burned, her hair was an unruly mess and she hadn't eaten.

She flicked on a light and shivered. The heating in the

Victorian took a long time to get going, so she left her jacket on and walked into the kitchen.

She intended to enjoy her dinner of a peanut butter sandwich and milk before taking a hot bath and collapsing beneath the thick down comforter on her bed.

In the upstairs bathroom, she discovered that the roof was leaking. With a scowl, she searched out a bucket and positioned it to catch the dripping water.

Great.

Shane was the only reputable contractor in town, and she needed him. Yet calling him was the last thing she wanted to do.

The leak could wait until tomorrow, she told herself.

Luckily, by the next morning, the leak had stopped completely and she put it out of her mind.

When she arrived at the old school building, her mouth fell open. Shane was there, a tool belt slung low around his hips and a black short-sleeved T-shirt conforming to his upper body. "I thought you were going to send over a crew."

He took in the way she was dressed, blue jeans, tennis shoes, a button-down shirt. She saw the approval in his forest-green eyes and felt a corresponding ripple of awareness in her stomach.

"Some of my men are out with the flu," he said.

"And you didn't want to disappoint the town."

"Something like that."

She wanted to push more but didn't dare. Instead, she asked, "What can I do to help?"

"Stay off ladders."

She looked at him, uncertain whether or not he was joking. He wasn't, she decided, judging by the look in his dark green eyes. "I want to help, and I will."

"This is my project now," he said. "I call the shots."

Her chin came up. "I'm paying the bills."

"And you're welcome to find another contractor."

"You're as stubborn as a mule," she said.

"Yeah," he agreed comfortably. "The mule who's in charge."

She squeezed her eyes shut. Things would be much easier with a contractor who didn't fill her mind with images of a lazy kiss and a roaring fire. "Let's call a truce," she said.

He arched an eyebrow.

"We need to work together, and I can't do it with all the tension that springs up every time we're alone. Let's forget that the weekend at your cabin ever happened and we can start over."

"Forget we kissed? Forget we made love?" he asked softly, his work boots echoing off the flooring and ricocheting from the ceiling as he moved toward her.

She stood her ground. "I can. Can you?"

"No."

Her knees weakened.

"I don't want to." He captured a lock of her hair and drew it toward him.

"Okay," she said, curling her hand around his wrist. "Don't forget it. We'll just call it what it was."

"And what was it?"

"Two adults with hormonal needs."

"Nothing more?"

She felt the thread of his pulse beneath her thumb, steady and strong. His skin was warm, and suddenly she was conscious of the intimacy. Quickly she released him. "Nothing more."

"Is that all it was to you?"

"Shane—"

"Was it?" he asked again.

He overwhelmed her senses. She saw only him, dressed in a black shirt and dark denim, smelled his citrusy aftershave, heard the slide of his baritone through her ears. The only thing missing was the taste of him, and heaven help her, she craved that, too.

"We didn't make love because we wanted it? Because it would be easier to forget to breathe than it would to be with each other?"

Needing the space, she put up a hand to stop him from coming closer. His heart thumped rhythmically beneath her palm. She grew warm, and her insides heated in response to him.

Matt knocked on the door and cleared his throat. She jumped back from Shane in relief. She was losing her mind....

Shane reluctantly let her go.

Her eyes were wide and luminous, her bottom lip damp where she'd moistened it.

After exchanging pleasantries with Matt, Angie excused them both and entered her office. Escaping? Shane wondered.

A few of his men arrived, and, needing the distraction himself, he got to work. At lunchtime, he went to the office, returned phone calls, checked his other job sites.

By the time he returned to the schoolhouse, the town's businesses were turning off lights and flipping their open signs to the closed side.

The Chuckwagon Diner had a waiting line, and Angie's car was the only one parked in front of the schoolhouse.

Damn it, she worked too hard. Always had. Trouble was, it irritated him as much now as it had five years ago. She thought it was about control, hadn't seen that it was more than that. He'd wanted to provide for his wife because he'd cared.

She was painting baseboard trim when he walked in.

Startled, she glanced up, eyes wide, her mouth forming a circle of surprise. "I didn't expect you to come back."

"The boss of this project is a slave driver, wants me to deliver on an impossible deadline."

"But she pays well." She grinned.

His eyes narrowed. "And works as hard as the crew."

She propped a hand on a hip. "You're not nagging me, are you?"

"Not as long as you're staying off ladders."

"I am."

His cellular phone rang, and under her breath Angie added, "When you're around."

"I heard that," he said, exchanging a glance with her. A small smile flirted with her lips. Before he could smile back, he turned to answer the call from his sister. When Sarah complained that she'd been trying to reach him at home and the office, he explained where he was.

"With Angie? Our Angie? For real? What's she doing back in town? Can I talk to her?"

His heart sank. In so many ways, he'd been hurt by Angie's desertion, but so had Sarah. She hadn't been old enough to remember their mother leaving, but the loss of Angie, so soon after their father's death, had spiraled Sarah into a funk for over a month.

"Come on, big brother. Let me talk to her."

Against his better judgment, he covered the mouthpiece. "Sarah wants to talk to you," he whispered to Angie.

"Sarah?" She dropped her paintbrush, hurriedly wiping her hands on her jeans. "I'd love to."

He didn't hand over the phone.

Angie met his gaze and tension crackled between them. He saw her face fall as she registered his expression. "You don't want me to talk to her."

"No."

"Then I won't."

"Sorry, sis, she's busy," he said to Sarah, steeling himself against the shadow of hurt in Angie's eyes. When she'd abandoned them, she'd made her choices. He knew women were all the same, that they ran at the first sign of trouble. Angie had hurt him and—more importantly—Sarah once. He'd be damned if he'd let it happen a second time.

Angie left the room and went into her office, quietly closing the door behind her.

He told himself it was better this way.

"She didn't want to talk to me, is that it?" Sarah asked.

"No," he assured his younger sister. "She's painting."

"Then I can call her back later?"

"That's not a good idea, Sarah."

"Are you trying to protect me, Shane?" she demanded. "I'm an adult now, you know."

"You're my little sister," he corrected her.

"If she doesn't want to talk to me, just say so."

He heard a mixture of pain and bravery skitter down her voice. "That's not it," he said.

"Then let me talk to her."

"Did you call for a reason?" he asked, raking his spread fingers through his hair. "Money?" he guessed.

"Are you changing the subject?" she asked suspiciously. "Why don't you want me to talk to her?"

"Sarah, she won't be here long."

"I can handle it, Shane. I love you, but you can't protect me forever."

But he wanted to, oh, how he wanted to.

"You said she didn't leave because of me."

"She didn't."

"Then I can still like her, can't I?"

How could he forget Sarah's tears and hurt? "It'd be easier if you didn't."

"Easier for who, Shane?" she asked quietly.

"For all of us."

"Are you okay with her being back?"

"Never better."

"Yeah," Sarah said disbelievingly, then she relented, telling Shane she had called for more money. She'd had to buy new clothes this semester, and did he have any idea how much they cost?

Shane said he'd take her word for it, promised to make a deposit in her account and hung up the phone, his gut tight. There'd been unmistakable excitement in Sarah's voice when she'd learned Angie was in town.

He thought of Angie's smile earlier and the way he'd responded to it. He recalled the way they'd teamed together the other day to paint her office, in perfect harmony.

He heard her moving around in the other room, and he pictured her as she had been earlier, bent over as she painted, her behind filling out her jeans, her breasts gently swaying with her motions. He swallowed.

Even though she wasn't intending to tempt him, Angie, just by being Angie, was insinuating herself back in his life and cracking the fortress he'd erected to keep her out. And Shane didn't like that.

He cleaned up the project he was working on, then headed out, not planning to tell her he was leaving.

"Are you going home?" she asked.

He turned. She stood in the office doorway, her shoulder propped against the jamb, paintbrush in hand and a smudge of paint on her right cheek. She looked alluring, but tired.

A part of him wanted to march in there and help her finish the job, then send her home where she could rest. But where Angie was concerned, he didn't dare be that noble. The other night's kiss had nearly undone him. He'd thought he'd exorcized her, that he was no longer weak where she was concerned.

Yet he was.

"How's Sarah?"

"Fine."

At his clipped answer, she blinked, but tried again. "Is she doing well at college?"

He nodded tightly.

"That's it? One-syllable answers, if you answer me at all?"

"What do you want from us, Angie?" he asked quietly, advancing a couple of steps toward her. He reminded himself who she really was. The woman who'd walked away from him, the woman who was leaving soon. "You waltz back into town and want to pick up where you left off. It won't work. We went on without you."

Her chin came up mutinously. "I missed Sarah."

"She cried for *you*, every night for a week."

Her voice was soft, trembly, when she said, "I cried for her, too."

"I won't let you back in our lives, Angie."

"I never meant to hurt her. Or you."

"Hurting me, I could have forgiven. I wouldn't have forgotten, but I might have forgiven. Hurting Sarah..."

He shook his head. "I blame myself, Angie. I knew you'd leave, just like everyone else did. I was a fool and took a chance. I had no right to do that, not to Sarah. I won't give you a second chance." Problem was, earlier, she'd tempted him again. It wasn't her that bothered him as much as his own reaction.

"Would it help you to know I'm sorry?"

"Save it for a guy who'll believe it." He turned on his heel and didn't look back.

Angie collapsed against the wall, exhaling in frustration. She'd thought she could work with Shane and keep the past buried, as if it had never happened. She now realized how ridiculous an idea that had been. There were too many raw wounds to pretend otherwise.

He carried emotional scars from her leaving, and he stubbornly refused to see that she'd intentionally hurt herself so he could keep his family intact. She didn't need a man like that in her life.

Angie had loved Sarah as if she were the sister Angie had never had. That summer, she had sat on Sarah's bed while Shane worked late. She'd painted a younger Sarah's toenails and listened to secrets about the boys at school.

When her father demanded Angie leave Colorado, anguish had nearly destroyed her. It hadn't been just Shane, it had been Sarah and Aunt Emma, too. Angie had left behind a town that felt like a family, a place where she'd belonged because of who she was, not because she was Edward Burton's daughter and an heiress.

The front door slammed and a car engine roared to life.

She was alone. Again.

Through the window, she watched Shane's taillights

disappear. Snow danced in the wind, playing beneath the streetlights. Except for her car, Front Street was deserted.

She cleaned up her painting supplies, then walked through the old building, turning off lights. As she did, she noticed the fresh paint and the walls he'd started to tear down that showed the project was progressing. Shane was doing a great job. She only wished her resolve to resist him was stronger....

She changed from her tennis shoes into boots and trudged to the Chuckwagon, a place she knew would be bustling with activity. She'd be able to forget the loneliness, or so she hoped.

All the tables were filled, so she took a seat at the long, scarred bar with short aluminum stools. The tops were covered with red, sparkly vinyl, with a few gashes in the fabric. She recalled them being exactly the same when she was here five years ago.

Bridget slid a cup of hot chocolate—complete with frothy whipped cream—in front of Angie.

"Nothing better when it's snowing, you know."

Angie smiled her thanks, then licked at the cream. As if it were yesterday, she remembered the time Shane had stopped by Aunt Emma's coffee shop, on his lunch break.

They'd been dating for a couple of weeks and he'd asked for a mocha latte, the only "fancy" coffee drink he knew. Angie had sprayed whipped cream all over the top, and when some dribbled down the side, she scooped it up with her finger and fed it to him. Afterward he'd admitted he'd only stopped by to see her. He'd won his first big construction bid and was anxious to share his success with her. She'd made herself a mocha latte also and they'd toasted his future. She was touched that he'd thought of her first, and he'd stolen a piece of her heart.

Part of her wondered if she'd ever really gotten it back....

"Do you mind if I sit here?" Bernadette asked.

"Be my guest," she said, grateful for the company and the interruption. "Beautiful flowers," she added, as Bernadette placed a carnation-filled vase between them.

"Yes, they are," she answered, rather dreamily, Angie thought.

The older woman seemed lost in thought as she fingered a pink bloom.

"Lillian Andrews makes me an arrangement each week."

"Always the same?"

Bernadette nodded. "Pink carnations."

Still spry at sixty-something, Bernadette wore her dark hair in a carefully coiffed bun, and her slim-fitting skirt was neatly pressed.

"Is there a reason they're always carnations?" Angie asked quietly.

"So I'll always remember," she said, then sighed. She blinked several times, then patted Angie's hand. "Enough about that." After smiling sunnily, she added, "Now, tell me, dear, are you settling in?"

"The house is big without Auntie Em."

"You'll just have to come back when she's here, then, won't you?"

Angie intended to come back for the center's grand opening, then stay away from Colorado—and Shane— for good. When she wanted to see Emma, Angie decided she'd fly her aunt to Chicago.

"I'll have to pop in and take a look at the remodeling project, if you don't mind. The town is quite excited, you know."

"So am I," Angie said, determinedly shoving

thoughts of Shane from her mind. "I love it when I can
see things progress and when I know it's going to be so
good for children. Aunt Emma was right, the town did
need it. I'm just glad I can help."

"And is Shane Masters doing the kind of job we all
promised you he would?"

If they only knew how personal the attention had gotten and how much it affected her... "He's on time and
under budget so far."

"And how are things between you and Shane?"

She blinked and sipped from the scalding drink,
avoiding Bernadette's eyes. "Shane and I were over five
years ago."

Bernadette tutted. "Is that why he was holding you
the other night?"

Angie nearly choked on her hot chocolate. Maybe the
town *did* know how personal Shane's attention was. She
hoped, though, that it didn't get reported in Miss Starr's
"Around the Town" newspaper column. "Holding
me?"

"Apparently a passerby saw you two through the
schoolhouse window Friday night."

"He was helping me down from a ladder."

"Oh, my! Were you going to fall?"

"I was fine." She shook her head. "Shane wasn't
convinced, though. He thinks he knows more than Dr.
Johnson about amnesia and my recovery."

"You know how these men are. Always the protec-
tor." She sighed wistfully. "He rescued you from the
storm, now from a ladder." Her eyes twinkled.

"There's nothing more to the story. Honest."

"If you say so, dear."

"You wouldn't be Miss Starr, would you?"

The woman waved a hand in front of her face.
"Mercy! Whatever makes you ask such a crazy thing?"

"You seem to have a real interest in the town's happenings."

"That I do. I do so love a love story, don't you?"

"As long as it happens to someone else."

"Such cynicism from such a young lady."

"What about you, Bernadette? Why aren't you involved in your own love story?"

"I was, once upon a time."

"And...?"

She patted her hair. "I'd have him in a minute, if he'd have me."

A part of Angie's heart softened. "Does he know that?" she asked gently.

"No."

"Maybe you should tell him."

"It's easier when you're younger, dear."

Before Angie could respond, Nick and Lilly Andrews came in for dinner with their infant, and Bernadette reintroduced Angie to the Andrewses.

Nick held his beautiful baby, Noelle, in his arms. Noelle slept peacefully, gently sucking her pacifier in her sleep. Angie couldn't help herself. She traced her finger across the baby's soft cheek, marveling at her perfection. "You're very lucky," Angie said quietly, looking up at Nick.

"I am," he agreed, his gaze connecting with his wife's. Their intimacy was deep and real, leaving Angie feeling like an outsider, even though she knew Lilly and Nick didn't mean to exclude her.

A moment later, while Bernadette and Nick were chatting, Lilly asked Angie, "How are you doing?"

"I'm recovered from the car accident."

"I meant, how are you doing with Shane?"

Angie's smile felt brittle. "I'll be going home soon."

"Shane's a friend."

"I know."

"But you are, also."

"Thank you."

"If you need someone to talk to…"

"Dinner's served," Bridget said, sliding fries and a sandwich in front of Angie and a gravy-rich chicken-fried steak in front of Bernadette.

The Andrewses excused themselves after Lilly invited Angie for dinner before she left town.

While they ate, Angie picking at her fries, Bernadette brought Angie up to date with the town's latest news.

"Perhaps you remember Jessica Majors—well, she would have been Jessica Stephens when you were here last—she's in the family way." Bernadette sounded quite satisfied. "That just leaves Shane and Slade Birmingham and our sheriff… Mercy. Well, it's high time our Shane had a family of his own. He's wonderful with his younger sister, but she's nearly all grown up. No doubt about it, our Shane will make a good daddy. I knew the same thing about Nicholas."

Angie rubbed at the sudden goose bumps on her arms. The idea of Shane and another woman having a baby made Angie cold.

When she left Shane and her life in Colorado, she'd known he might remarry and have a family. So why did the thought of him with another woman now bother her so much? And why was she suddenly picturing herself cradling Shane's baby in her arms?

Angie shook her head, determined to push aside that tempting image. Her work with children satisfied her maternal instincts. Not having anyone tell her what to do made her happy.

Or she thought it had, until this moment.

"Don't you agree, dear?"

"Agree?"

"That Shane will be a wonderful daddy?"

Bernadette was right. "Yes," Angie answered. He *would* be a wonderful father, but it wouldn't be to her child.

She lost the rest of her appetite and didn't respond when Bernadette scolded her for eating like a bird.

After paying her bill, Angie huddled against the cold and hurried back to her car. The more she thought about Shane, the more she realized she needed to get back to Chicago and her real life.

Must be something about the town, she decided. Maybe it was the lack of oxygen at this altitude that made her forget everything except the fact she and Shane worked together incredibly well and that he was a sexy man and she still desired him....

She drove home on the slick roads, trying to block out images of Shane cradling his child the way she'd seen Nick hold his.

Big, fat flakes still drifted from the sky, and more were promised. She slid through an intersection and was wishing for summer by the time she reached the Victorian.

Inside she heard a steady drip, and she followed the sound to the upstairs bathroom. Angie groaned. The roof was leaking again and the bucket she'd positioned had spilled over. Much as she hated to call Shane, she needed his advice.

Trying to still her racing pulse, she looked up his name in the directory and dialed his number.

After four rings, the answering machine picked up.

As she debated whether or not to leave a message, another large drop of water splashed into the bucket, then onto the floor. The moment she started speaking, he answered.

Just the sound of his voice, rich and thick, chased fresh goose bumps up her arms.

"What can I do for you?" he asked.

She wound her finger into the phone cord. "My roof is leaking."

"At the center?"

"No, at my aunt's house."

"When did it start?"

"I noticed it yesterday morning."

"And you didn't tell me?"

"It had stopped this morning, so I thought—"

"I'll be there in ten minutes."

"Shane, really, I'm sure it'll be okay—"

"Ten minutes." With that, he hung up.

While she impatiently waited, she brewed a pot of coffee, cleaned up the water mess, turned up the heat a few degrees and looked out the window half a dozen times. She saw the headlights of Shane's four-wheel-drive vehicle in nine minutes.

She answered the door, saying, "I appreciate your coming over, but it really wasn't necessary."

"Yeah, I know." He stamped his feet, flinging snow on the porch. He shucked out of his coat at the same moment she closed the door. "Sorry," he said, grabbing her shoulders as he bumped into her.

It was okay, except for the fact she could no longer think. Since their kiss she'd been hypersensitive to him, every nerve ending on a low simmer of awareness.

For a second neither said anything, and she heard the

pounding of her own heart. She wished she hadn't turned up the heat, because the house suddenly felt like a tropical rain forest. "I made coffee."

He nodded. "Where's the leak?"

"Upstairs bathroom."

Shane released her and she escaped to the kitchen. Even though she didn't want a cup of coffee, she poured one for herself and one for Shane. Holding it would occupy her hands.

She started toward the stairs the moment Shane started down them.

"You can't stay here."

"It's not that bad."

He raised a brow.

"Is it?"

"How long has it been since your aunt had her roof replaced?"

"I'm not sure."

"Come here."

Mouth dry, she followed him up the stairs. The bathroom seemed much smaller with Shane's large body filling it.

He pointed to the ceiling and she slid both mugs of coffee onto the vanity. "See that huge water spot?"

She nodded.

"The ceiling is sagging. Pack enough clothes for a couple of days."

Her mouth gaped. "I beg your pardon?"

"You can have my bedroom. I'll take the couch."

She shook her head. "I'm staying here."

"Not until I've fixed the problem."

"The leak isn't that bad."

He folded his arms across his chest, and his dark green

eyes flashed determination. "You're coming home with me. Pack a bag, or I'll pack it for you."

"Forget it, Shane." She folded her own arms and stood her ground. "This is my decision."

"It's my responsibility," he countered. "You called me. In my professional opinion, the roof is structurally unsound. I won't gamble with your life."

"You're being melodramatic."

The determination in his eyes became a dare. "Pack a bag, Angie."

"Not interested, thank you."

With a curt nod, he reacted, swallowing the distance to her bedroom in a handful of strides.

Angie was hot on his heels. "What do you think you're doing?"

He yanked open the closet door and grabbed a small bag. "Taking you home with me."

"You can't."

"Watch me."

He opened a drawer and pulled out a couple of pairs of panties and a bra and started tossing them into the bag. She grabbed his wrist, insisting, "Stop that immediately."

He seared her with his gaze.

She shivered.

"You've got two choices, lady. Pack this damn bag or I'll pack it for you." Even with a pair of her silky panties hooked on his thumb, he'd never looked more serious.

"If it doesn't stop leaking, I'll go to the Hot Springs Resort tomorrow."

"Heard the weather report?"

She felt the rhythmic and strong beat of his pulse beneath her fingertips.

"Five more inches of snow," he said quietly. "Know how heavy that is?"

Darn him, he had a point.

"The roof could come down while you're in the bathtub."

She could be persuaded with logic, but not by his domineering male act.

When he spoke again, his voice had softened, and despite herself, her resistance waned. "Do it for your aunt. She'd be devastated if something happened to you."

Would he? she wondered. "You're right," she said, letting go of his wrist.

"You'll finish packing?"

If it got him out of here, away from the bed, she'd do anything. "Yes."

"I'll be downstairs."

"I'll drive my own car."

"Fine. I'll still wait."

She nodded. He dropped her panties on top of the bra and left the room, and his clean, crisp scent still stamped the air.

Angie sighed. What had she gotten herself into with Shane, and how would she survive being at his house?

Ten

The storm had frozen his brain cells. No doubt about it.

Shane punched his pillow. He'd had enough of Angie after her car accident. So why the hell had he insisted on bringing her back here?

Damn his sense of responsibility, anyway.

He thumped the pillow again, ignoring the nagging voice that whispered he hadn't helped her because of a sense of responsibility. He'd helped dozens of women in the past. But he hadn't brought one of them to his house, let alone insisted they sleep in his bed.

Angie had called him for help and he'd charged off, simple as that. All that was missing was a white horse.

There was something about the core of vulnerability that she tried to hide behind a veneer of independence. Shane wondered if he was trying to prove to her that she needed him as much as he desired her.

Hardhat slunk a couple of inches closer to the fire-place's dying embers, and Shane pulled off his shirt. Maybe the night air would help cool his heated skin.

Giving up the battle, he succumbed to a sleep haunted by images of his ex-wife.

Moments, or hours later, he woke up to see her standing near the back of the house, at the sliding glass door, staring into the stormy night. Grabbing his shirt, he swung his legs off the couch and moved toward her. "Angie? What are you doing?"

Jumping a bit, she turned to face him, her palm pressing against the pulse in her throat. "Hardhat wanted to go out."

"Hardhat?"

She smiled a little, dropping her hand. "I think he got tired of trying to wake you up."

So much for Shane's protective instincts...

Hardhat pushed his nose against the door and barked once. Angie let him back in, then wrapped her arms beneath her breasts. The motion stretched her long cotton gown taut, revealing her thickened nipples. Shane's throat was suddenly parched.

The glow from a dim lamp silhouetted her feminine form, and he couldn't help but notice her pink-painted toenails peeking from beneath the hem of her gown. Her hair framed her face, loose and free, making him wish he'd been the one to muss it up.

The open neckline of her gown had exposed part of her upper chest, and Shane couldn't help but notice the creaminess of her skin. She was every bit as alluring to him as she'd been the first night they'd made love, five years before.

He wanted to touch her but didn't dare. If he started, he wasn't sure he could stop.

"Sorry the mutt woke you up. Thought he had better manners than that."

"I couldn't sleep, anyway." She met his gaze. "You can have your bed back, if you'd like. At least one of us should rest."

"I told you, the bed's yours."

"Yes, I know."

"You don't like anyone telling you what to do," he stated.

"No."

"Not even when it's for your own good."

"Especially when it's for my own good," she replied. "Sorry we disturbed you, Shane. Go back to sleep."

He should. Rational thought told him exactly that. But he didn't.

When she started to move past him, he captured her upper arm, stopping her. "Tell me why, Angie."

"There's nothing to tell."

"You weren't this way when we were married."

"What way?"

"Distant. Distrustful."

She looked at him and said, "Experience."

He heard the bitterness she tried to hide. "You refuse to listen to anything I say."

"I like my independence."

"What are you afraid of?"

"I'm not afraid," she snapped back.

"Then why didn't you want to come here?"

"Because you demanded it. You didn't ask what I wanted. You assumed you knew what was best." She moved his hand from her arm. "I swore I'd never answer to another man again."

"Swore? To whom?"

"To myself."

He dropped his arms to his sides and reluctantly let her move away. It was one of the hardest things he'd done. He wanted answers, wanted to understand.

She moved toward the window, and he saw her shiver.

Needing something to do, he started a fire and drummed his fingers on the mantel as he struggled to find some patience.

"You still may think I left willingly, that I wanted to marry Jack Hague, but I didn't."

His jaw tightened.

She turned and faced him. "You asked, Shane. Do you want the truth, or do you want to forget you asked?"

She tipped her chin back. "I can go either way," she said. Her blue eyes flashed with fire, and he had no doubt this wasn't the same woman who'd left him.

"Give me the truth."

"Jack and I fought the day I got back to town. He told me to take off the aspen leaf. I refused. That set the tone for our relationship."

"You kept it on while you were married?"

"Yes."

"Even when you made love?"

"We didn't."

His mind swam. "You didn't make love?"

"No."

He felt as if he'd been knocked in the back of the head with a two-by-four. "Never?"

She pulled back her shoulders, but he saw telltale flushes of red highlighting her cheeks, showing him she'd been hurt, despite her determination to hide the truth.

"In three years of marriage, you never once made love?"

Angie shook her head. "Even though Jack knew I wanted children."

"Son of a bitch."

"He said we might have kids, eventually. But first, he'd have to learn to trust me. You see, I'd betrayed him with you."

His chest constricted. "You weren't engaged to him when you moved here."

"I knew it was my dad's expectation, but I'd never agreed. Dad never told Jack that you and I had married."

He heard the catch in her voice as she continued. "When he saw the aspen leaf, he asked about it. I told him about you, our life together, and he called me a whore, said I'd betrayed him. Luckily for me, he said, he wanted the business deal badly enough not to let the fact I was soiled goods stand in the way."

Soiled goods? Raw energy churning in his gut, Shane paced the living room. For the past five years, he'd been focused on his own pain, on her betrayal of their vows. He'd never really believed she hadn't had any options. Until now, he hadn't calculated the cost to her.

Maybe she wasn't the woman he'd believed her to be. Maybe she wasn't as cold and callous as he thought....

She put her hands to her face for a second, before looking at him. "I spent my marriage trying to atone for a sin I didn't realize I'd committed.

"Jack led me to believe that we'd have children, as long as I toed the line he drew. He told me he didn't want me working—said it would be better for our children if I raised them myself. I agreed with that, but I couldn't handle shopping and doing nothing all day, so I got involved with a couple different children's charities."

"I saw you with the kids at the community center."

"I love them all."

"Yeah. It shows."

"That's the best thing that came out of my marriage. But now, looking back, I can't believe I allowed him to dictate my life." She shook her head. "I was an idiot. He told me what to do, and I did it. I tried to make the best of my marriage. I figured I was stuck with it and intended to honor my vows." Unwaveringly she fixed her gaze on him. When she spoke again, there was underlying steel in her voice. "No matter what you believe about me, Shane, I didn't walk away from you."

"He punished you."

"Yes."

He plowed his hands through his hair, trying to make sense of it all.

But she wasn't finished. "At Jack's funeral, I came face-to-face with his mistress and their ten-month-old baby."

He stopped pacing and ground his back teeth.

"He gave her what he'd never given me."

Without conscious thought, he crossed to her.

"Marcy said he was a good dad to his son, said that Jack intended to include them in his will and make Jack Junior his heir when my father died."

Her voice had changed, becoming hoarser, and Shane felt a corresponding softening in his heart. He took her shoulders in his hands and held her gently.

"Ironic, isn't it? He believed I betrayed him. You believed I betrayed you. And the only thing I ever wanted to do was the right thing."

A gentleness he was unfamiliar with overtook Shane. He stroked Angie's hair, feathering the silky strands away from her cheeks, then cradled her face. He'd spent the last five years thinking. Now he simply felt.

She looked at him, her blue eyes wide. They telegraphed honesty. Eyes were a window and they never lied; he knew that.

"There's never been anyone but you, Shane."

Passion, as deeply emotional as physical, flared in him. He claimed her lips, tasting and taking.

She didn't just respond; instead she met his kiss with a demand.

She grabbed at his shirt, shoving the material from his shoulders and dropping it to the hardwood floor.

He pulled at the satin string holding her gown closed.

Her hands were on his chest, her fingers tangling in the scattering of soft hair, then moving downward.

Their kiss deepened, and their tongues thrust against each other's in a simulated love dance.

She tugged at the snap holding his jeans closed. He sucked in his breath when she found the zipper. She started to pull on the small tab, and he instantly hardened.

He ended the kiss. Even to his own ears, his voice sounded raw when he said, "I want to see you undressed."

"You, too," she said.

His pulse surged. He snagged her gown and drew it over her head.

She stood before him, her back to the hearth. The firelight flickered off the golden highlights in her hair. "You're lovely."

"Your turn," she said.

In seconds, he'd undressed, dropping his clothes in a pile near hers.

He heard her breath hitch, and his manhood pulsed in response.

He dropped to his knees in front of her and cupped

her buttocks, then placed a kiss right below her belly button. Her hands dug into his hair. He moved slightly lower and kissed her once more, then again, lower still. When her knees buckled, he caught her and eased her down beside him. "Open your legs for me."

She did, and he placed a hand between her legs, touching her. With a gasp, she leaned closer to him and his finger slipped against her flesh. She was moist and he could no longer wait.

"Now, Shane," she said.

"Here?"

"Yes," she whispered.

In seconds, he'd lowered her to the floor and propped a pillow beneath her head. He paused before entering her, looking at her expression and again realizing he was her only one.

Emotion shuddered through him. This time, there was no past, no regrets, and he held nothing back as he made love to her like he hadn't since the day she left.

This was the way it should have been, the way it might have been, if only she hadn't left him....

"Where are you going?"

His voice, hoarse and sexy, sent a skitter up her spine. "I'm not going anywhere," she said softly. "I was just stretching."

"Good," he said with a half smile.

She didn't think he'd even woken up all the way, but that didn't stop him from placing a hand on the small of her back and bringing her back against him. There was a time she imagined being with him like this always.

After their lovemaking, Shane had carried her to bed and folded her protectively in his arms. He'd promised to keep her warm, saying she didn't need her night-clothes.

Beneath the down comforter, she'd snuggled against him, bare skin to bare skin, one of her palms resting on his chest, her head in that tender spot between his shoulder and arm.

He'd fallen asleep almost instantly and had never released his hold on her. She, on the other hand, hadn't even closed her eyes.

She wondered what she was doing here, wondered why she'd agreed to come home with him, wondered why she'd surrendered so completely to him.

Shane spelled *danger* in capital letters. It had taken her a long time to get over him, and opening herself like this would only make it more difficult to leave town forever.

He moved, and she felt him against her, hard again.

"Keep still," he muttered. "Unless…"

"Unless?" she asked breathlessly.

And he showed her…

Angie didn't get a lot more sleep the rest of the night, but she wasn't complaining.

The next morning the phone rang. He placed a gentle kiss on her nose before picking up the receiver.

While he was on the phone, she dressed and went into the kitchen, finding eggs and milk in the refrigerator.

She hummed while she assembled ingredients on the counter. There was something homey about being in his kitchen, wearing one of his shirts over her jeans, the muffled sound of his rich baritone from the other room, the warmth of the heat whispering from the vents, the scent of brewing coffee, the sight of Hardhat with his head cocked to one side expectantly. She liked the feeling of comfort and welcome.

She heard his quiet approach on bare feet.

"Hungry?" she asked, pouring egg batter into a heated skillet.

Shane came up behind her and gently drew her back against him. He nuzzled her neck. "Yeah."

"I'm talking about breakfast."

"So was I."

"I'll bet," she said, wriggling in his arms so that she could look at him. "So what kind of eggs were you talking about?"

"Eggs?"

"Breakfast, remember?"

"Okay, okay," he admitted. With his hands on her shoulders, he nudged her a bit closer to him. "So I wasn't talking about food."

"Didn't think so," she said, feeling the proof that he wasn't interested in eggs, or the toast and coffee she'd put on. She reached up to stroke his shadowed cheek, and she familiarly rested her finger in the cleft of his chin. He'd become so important to her in such a short time. How was that possible? "But the omelette will burn if you keep this up."

"Does it matter?"

"No. But the smoke detector might ruin the mood."

"I'll settle for a kiss, for now."

But it wasn't just any kiss...it was a joining that made her knees weaken.

"That'll hold me," he said.

She could barely think.

While he poured coffee, she served the omelette...nearly dropping the spatula when he stroked her spine.

''This is wonderful,'' he said when they were sitting across from each other at the intimately small table. Their knees brushed, and he raised his brow. A warmth flooded through her, making her hot.

She wanted to be immune to Shane, and, just as certainly, she wasn't.

''Where did you learn to cook?''

She tried to focus on the mundane, rather than the effect he was having over her. It was powerful and seductive, and she knew she had to fight it.

She was falling for Shane again and that was the one thing she dared not do. A relationship with her ex-husband was impossible. He didn't trust her, wouldn't trust her and she had her own life. So why couldn't she seem to help herself?

''Cooking was one of my escapes. We had a wonderful housekeeper who cooked our meals. When Jack wasn't home, I spent time in the kitchen with Carmen. She taught me everything I know. I make a wonderful chicken enchilada dish.''

''You'll have to make it for me.''

For the first time, he hinted at a future, and her stomach tightened. She pushed part of her omelette around her plate. A future was impossible. She had a separate life—a life she liked—and didn't intend to give it up.

She wondered why that thought wasn't as appealing as it had been even a week ago.

''That was Sarah on the phone earlier,'' he said quietly.

She wasn't surprised he didn't let her talk to his sister, but the hurt was still there, a reminder he didn't intend to share his life with her.

''She said she's coming home for a while.''

"Oh?" She put down her fork, trying not to let it clatter.

"I said you two could talk. She said she'd rather say hello in person."

Her pulse completely missed its next beat. "You offered?"

"Yeah. I figured she needed to know you'd be here."

She looked at Shane. Her heart in her throat she asked, "Do you want me to leave?"

"No."

"Are you sure?"

He put down his own utensils and looked at her unflinchingly. "You need a place to stay."

Simple as that. Regardless, she wanted to see Sarah and appreciated his small offer of trust. "Thank you."

For a second, expectancy pulsed. "You're welcome," he said sincerely. Her heart missed a beat. Then he stood and grabbed his plate. "She's got a surprise. Last time she had a surprise, she'd bought me a power tool."

"That was nice." Angie's mind raced as she struggled to keep up.

"And she brought me the bill."

Angie laughed and joined him at the sink. "Let me guess, you told her thanks."

"She had good intentions."

"You made Sarah a great older brother." She placed her fingers on his arm. "I knew you would."

"I tried."

"It's the best we can all do." Softly she added, "It's all I ever did."

Together they cleaned the kitchen, and Angie was lost in her thoughts.

She wondered if she'd made all the right choices in her life. She'd spent a couple of years avoiding men, convinced they were all like Jack and her father. Even Shane wanted to tell her what to do, but it was different, somehow. Being with him here didn't seem like the shackle she feared it would be.

This morning, she'd slowly awakened and realized she liked the protective feel of his arms around her. Drying dishes that he rinsed, working in partnership, she wondered if being alone was as wonderful as she'd been telling herself it was.

"Sarah should be here this afternoon. I figure we can come home early." He glanced at the clock. "And we've got an hour before we need to be at work."

"What did you have in mind?"

He leaned over and whispered.

His breath tickled her ear; the suggestion tightened her tummy. "Really?" she asked.

"Unless you have a better idea?"

She didn't.

Eleven

"**Y**ou're engaged?" Shane demanded of his sister.

Angie wrapped her arms around herself, seeing fire flash in Shane's darkened eyes.

Sarah, on the other hand, was oblivious. She extended her hand toward Angie and turned her ring finger so the diamond caught the light. "Isn't the ring beautiful?"

"It's—"

Shane interrupted her answer with a scowl and sharp shake of his head. Angie's heart sank. Sarah's excitement was palpable, and Angie all too well remembered feeling the same way herself, five long and lonely years ago.

"Oh, I'm so glad you're here, Angie. It's awesome to get to see you and to have you share this with us."

Sarah threw her arms around Angie and squeezed tight. Over the younger woman's shoulders, Angie saw Shane fold his arms across his chest. His eyebrows had furrowed into a straight line. She shivered, remembering the same expression when he realized she'd gotten her memory back.

When Sarah had called the other day, he'd made it clear that he didn't want Angie to be part of their lives. Standing here, in Shane's house, she was never more conscious of being an outsider, and she'd never wanted to be an insider more.

Sarah released Angie and spun around. "You're going to love Mondo, Shane. He's just the coolest."

"Mondo?"

"Oh, that's just his biker name. His real name is Kevin."

"His biker name?" Shane asked, his voice deadly quiet.

"Oh, he rides a motorcycle. Wait till you get a load of it. It's like really cool."

"Sit down, Sarah."

Sarah blinked and looked to Angie for reassurance. Angie exhaled and gave Sarah a quick smile.

"I said sit down."

Her smile fell. "What do you want to know?"

"Where did you meet this boy?"

"He's a man, not a boy."

"And where did you meet him?" Shane repeated.

A band tightened around Angie's heart. This conversation was so familiar. Her father had badgered her and she'd been helpless to fight him. She'd been devastated when she saw her father wasn't happy for her, destroyed when she realized he would stop at nothing to make sure she didn't stay with Shane.

"When is this marriage planned? After graduation?"

"Now."

"Now?" he echoed.

"That's why I'm here. I wanted to tell you and, you know, invite you to the wedding, if you want to go. We're going to Vegas. Then we're going to spend the next few months traveling around the country on his bike."

"Over my dead body."

Angie's pulse slowed and she sank onto the edge of a chair near the fireplace. The past was repeating itself. The players were different, but the story was the same, the words nearly identical. He had to see... "Shane—"

He cut her a warning glance but said nothing.

"You don't want to go to my wedding?" Sarah asked, her lower lip trembling.

"There isn't going to be a wedding."

Sarah's chin tipped defiantly. "Oh, yes, there is."

"I forbid it."

"Forbid it?" She jumped up. "You forbid it?"

Angie saw an ominous ticking in his temple. From experience, she could read it. Shane had a short leash on his temper, and it was threatening to unravel. "You need to finish your education."

"I'm dropping out."

Silence shuddered. "You're too young to get married."

"That's rich, Shane. How old were you when you and Angie got married?"

"My marriage isn't the issue."

"Of course it isn't. Do as I say, not as I do. Is that right, big brother? Well I'll tell you what. I don't need your permission to get married. I'm an adult."

"You're a kid."

Tears trembled on Sarah's lashes. Angie couldn't sit still another moment. She moved across the room to where Shane stood and gently touched his shoulder.

He rounded on her. "This is between me and my sister."

"I know. But—"

Sarah, tears now spilling, said, "Don't bother, Angie. He's being a jerk and I don't have to listen to him."

"Sarah—" Shane said with a low growl.

"I'm out of here." She pivoted and stormed toward the door. "Have a good life, big brother."

"Where the hell do you think you're going?"

"Away. Away from you, away from this backward town."

Angie saw pain sketch across his eyes, leaving a trail of darkness in the deep green color.

There was resolve in the set of his shoulders, weariness in his voice, when he said, "If you leave, don't come back."

Angie gasped and grabbed Shane's arm. Tears stung her own eyes. "You don't mean it. Tell her you don't mean it."

Sarah paused, her hand on the front doorknob, and looked over her shoulder. "I hoped you'd be happy for me. I packed up all my stuff and brought it home in my car. I was hoping to leave everything here while we traveled. I was counting on you. Dumb, huh?"

Angie read the haunted look in the younger woman's eyes. She desperately wanted to be reassured, desperately wanted love. Angie had been there herself, knew how Sarah felt.

"Damn it, Shane." Angie shook his arm. "Don't do this to your sister," she insisted. "She's all you've got left."

"Women always leave. Why the hell would I think she'd be any different?"

Her stomach plummeted. Shane wasn't going to stop

his sister from leaving. In fact, he was shoving her away. His jaw was tight and he'd already hardened his heart against any more hurt, the exact same way he'd closed her off.

Angie squeezed her eyes shut.

"Have a good life. Mondo's waiting in town." Sarah slammed the door behind her.

Hardhat tipped his head to one side, then crossed to Shane, nuzzling his hand with a soft whimper.

Shane just stood there, pain obviously holding him immobile.

Angie knew there was no way she could stand back and watch Shane's anguish cost him his sister.

At a run, she chased after Sarah. Even though she nearly lost her balance on a patch of ice, Angie hurried through the snow, finally catching Sarah at her car.

"Wait," Angie said, positioning herself so Sarah couldn't slam the door closed.

"What's the point?"

In Sarah's eyes, Angie saw a reflection of herself several years ago, a young woman who knew what she wanted, torn between the two men she loved. She ached for Sarah, ached for her own losses. "Running won't solve anything. I promise you. I've learned that the hard way."

"Shane doesn't care about anything but having his own way. He's always been like this. You know that. He likes telling everyone what to do. Shane always knows best. At least that's what he thinks. Jerk."

"He isn't a jerk, Sarah. He loves you."

"I heard the two of you fight a few times. You didn't like him telling you what to do, either. Isn't that why you left?"

Angie rubbed her arms, trying to stay warm in the

frosty bite of mountain air. "No. I left because my father didn't give me a choice. My father wanted me to marry his business associate. He threatened to ruin Shane and make sure you and Shane were separated. I couldn't let that happen."

"And what did Shane say? Didn't he tell you to stay, that he could fix everything?"

"I never told him."

"Why not? Because he would have told you what to do, right? Man, he thinks he's always right." Sarah swiped at her tears and started the car engine.

"Listen to me," Angie implored. "Shane only wants what's best for you."

"Like your father wanted what was best for you? As if you didn't know what you wanted? Well, I'm not you. I'm not going to be pushed around by any guy. Me and Mondo are going to have a great life."

"Are you sure about that?"

She set her chin stubbornly. "Positive."

Angie could remember herself, so young, so sure. Now she had more questions than answers.... "Where are you going to live?"

"We're going to travel."

"And after that?"

"We'll find someplace."

"Does Mondo have a house? An apartment?"

"We'll get one later."

"So he doesn't have a job?"

"We'll earn enough to get by."

The night time cold gnawed on Angie's earlobes, but this was too important for her to give up. Softly she asked, "Is this the kind of life you really want for yourself? Do you really want to cut yourself off from Shane, to ignore his birthday and holidays, to pretend you didn't have all those wonderful years together?''

And she thought of her own sacrifice, walking away so that Shane and his sister would have the chance to be a family. She couldn't stand to see that thrown away.

"He doesn't care about me, only that I live up to his rules. As long as he's the boss and I say yes sir, no sir, everything's fine."

"Is that really true?" Angie's breath hung on the air. "Do you really not want to see your brother again, after all the years you two were alone? Think about it, Sarah, please. Shane loves you."

She dropped her head onto the steering wheel. "He has a funny way of showing it."

"He's not perfect, but he's doing the best he can. Don't go, Sarah, at least not until the two of you have a chance to talk."

"And what if he won't listen?"

"At least you will have tried. Do this for yourself, if not for your brother. Don't cut yourself off, Sarah." Quietly, she spoke from her own pain. "You can't undo the past and change things."

"He told me to leave."

"And he didn't mean it. Try. Please try."

Sarah looked up at Angie. "Will you talk to him?"

"I'll ask him to hear you out."

"Okay." Her face tear-stained, Sarah nodded. "Mondo and I will be at the Chuckwagon Diner, if Shane wants to come and find us."

Angie sighed and gave a little smile, showing a belief she didn't feel. Shane wasn't likely to listen to her— she'd seen the resolve in the set of his lips. He loved his sister; of that Angie had no doubt. But he didn't have much faith in women, and he rightly blamed part of that on her. Still, she had to try....

She trudged back through the snow and found Shane inside, his arms still folded as he stared into the crackling fire.

She stopped halfway into the room, knowing he'd heard her enter. He didn't acknowledge her. Her fingers were frozen from being outside so long, and Shane's reception chilled her the rest of the way to the bone. "Why are you hardening your heart against your sister?" she asked quietly.

He didn't answer.

"You're pushing her away, severing the relationship so that you don't get hurt any worse than you already are. Is that it, Shane? You're afraid of being hurt, so you'd prefer to make it simpler and less painful by sending Sarah away."

He swung around to face her. Lines were grooved deeply beside his eyes and anger emanated from him like a winter storm. "You don't know what the hell you're talking about."

"I know exactly what I'm talking about," she contradicted him. Her heart thundered.

"This is between me and my sister." He took a menacing step toward her, but she stood her ground. "This is none of your business. If you'll remember, you made the decision to walk out. You chose not to be part of this family."

"That's not true." A lump formed in her throat and she swallowed it back. "If I had come to you with my father's ultimatum, you would have reacted the same way you just did with Sarah. You closed yourself off to love because you're afraid of pain." And she could no longer be around him. "But I'll tell you this...the only thing you've really done is shut yourself off to the joys of life. Sorrow always comes and it doesn't hurt any less because you've hardened your heart. You care, Shane. I know you do.

"And you still have a chance with your sister. She and Mondo will be at the Chuckwagon Diner. I don't know how long they'll wait. But if you go, try shutting your mouth and listening. You're behaving like my father did. And look what it did to us." Drawing a breath, she added, "Don't let your fear ruin this relationship."

Shutters had dropped over his eyes. He looked cold and remote, as silent as the mountain peaks surrounding them. "Is that all?"

"I'm leaving."

"I won't let you stay in that house."

"Give me some credit, Shane. I'm going to the Hot Springs Resort. I wouldn't go to my aunt's to spite you." She hurried into his bedroom and grabbed her overnight bag, trying to pretend her hands weren't shaking as she tossed in her clothes and toiletries.

It was better this way, she told herself. She couldn't stay with a man who shut himself off to the world, who'd rather hurt than be hurt. In making love with him, she'd already exposed herself, becoming vulnerable to him.

She jerked closed the zipper to her bag and squared her shoulders when she went back into the living room.

Wordlessly, Shane watched her leave, his eyes narrowed, his arms folded uncompromisingly across his chest.

She tossed her bag in the car, then slammed the door and drove toward town, hoping there were rooms available at the Hot Springs Resort.

Things were impossible with Shane, she realized.

Even now, he hadn't given an inch. He hadn't tried to stop her from leaving; he'd stood there and watched her walk out.

Beneath the tree where he'd proposed to her, the same place she'd slid off the road and lost her memory, she stopped and gave into the tears she could not hold back any longer.

Earlier she'd been thinking that maybe she'd made the wrong choices in her life. Now she was grateful she had her own life.

Being alone didn't hurt as much as caring did.

She loved her work with kids. She was making a difference in the world. She was completely satisfied.

Why, then, did tears burn her eyes?

If life with Shane was impossible, why did her heart feel as though it had a hole in the bottom? And why did she want, more than anything else, to be in his arms?

A tear slid from her eye and splashed onto the steering wheel as she left him forever.

Energy, raw and restless, churned in Shane's gut.

Damn it. Damn her.

He slammed his fist into his open palm. It was better that Angie was gone. She intended to leave town, anyway. The sooner the better. She'd been insinuating herself back into his life. No, better that she'd left now. He should have never brought her back to the house last night.

That was the problem with Angie. He didn't have a hell of a lot of willpower when it came to her. She had a way of firing all his protective impulses, and she sure as moonlight didn't want them.

She was part of his past and should stay there.

But damned if he could banish the memory of her.

The room smelled of her light perfume and the pillows were scattered on the floor from their earlier lovemaking. He thought of their breakfast conversation, their laughter and the way she'd honestly shared the secrets of her past. And more, he recalled their times together...the way they worked together at the community center, the way she always took time for the kids who called her Angel.

If what Angie said was true—and the more he was around her, the more he believed her—she'd left him so he wouldn't lose Sarah. And now, Angie had stood up to him again, trying to make sure he didn't lose Sarah.

In frustration, he raked his hands through his hair.

Sarah's and Angie's leaving turned him upside down. He thought of Angie's dedication to the town and to kids. Much as he didn't want to admit it, Angie had been right about a few things. He didn't want to lose his sister. He didn't want Sarah making any foolish mistakes. God knew, he'd made enough for both of them.

But when it came down to it, she was family and he wanted her in his life.

To hell with being hurt, he wanted to live.

Hardhat padded over and nuzzled Shane. "What do you think, boy? Too quiet around here?"

Hardhat barked.

Decision made, he grabbed his car keys and Hardhat bounded toward the door, excited for the drive to town. The dog scrabbled into the car and stuck his nose against the passenger window.

Shane slowed as he neared the tree where he'd proposed to Angie. There were fresh tire tracks in the snow and an indentation in the mud beneath where the back tires had obviously spun when the vehicle left. She'd been here, no doubt. But why? Why would their past have mattered to her?

Lost in his own thoughts, he drove the rest of the way with the radio turned off and nothing but Hardhat's occasional sounds to break the silence.

He saw his sister's car parked along Front Street.

Sighing with relief, he went inside the Chuckwagon while Hardhat curled up on the blanket in the back seat.

Mondo—at least Shane assumed it was Mondo since the guy was sitting next to Sarah and eating off her plate—didn't look as bad as Shane feared. Yeah, he wore a leather jacket and had hair that stood straight up, but there wasn't any metal hanging from the guy's nose or ears. And his hair was plain brown—no pink or blue in sight. He looked more like a Kevin than a Mondo. Shane thanked his lucky stars.

He started across to the booth and Bridget called out a greeting. He responded and Sarah's head snapped up. Her gaze fastened on his and she blinked a few times. Instinctively she reached for Mondo's hand. Mondo put his arm around her, protectively drawing her closer to him. Obviously their relationship had developed deeper than Shane would have imagined possible.

"I didn't think you'd come," she said, her voice cracking with nerves when he slid into the booth across from the young couple.

"You're my sister," he said simply, profoundly.

"Does that mean you're not kicking me out of your life?"

He winced. "It means I owe you an apology."

"What?" Her mouth fell open.

"I should hear you out, listen to your plans, not shut you out. It means…" He cleared his throat. "I apologize."

"You're not very good at that."

"Haven't had much practice."

"It's accepted." Sarah smiled and this time reached for his hand, giving it a reassuring squeeze. "I love you, too, Shane. And I don't want to lose you."

"That's what I meant."

"I know." Sarah sipped from her straw. "I'd like you to meet my fiancé, Mondo."

The younger man extended his hand and Shane shook it.

"Hey, man, I'm not, you know, out to take your sister away from you." He raised his hands, as if in surrender. "I don't mean you any trouble."

All too clearly, he saw the similarities Angie had been talking about earlier. Just like a younger Angie had loved him, Sarah loved Mondo. It didn't matter that Shane would have chosen a different type of man for his little sister. And he suddenly wondered, would he think any man would be good enough for her?

Had Angie's father felt the same way? Edward Burton hadn't known Shane. The man had probably taken a look at Shane's background, the cabin, his barely-scraping-by business and decided he wasn't good enough for Angie. Though Edward Burton was guilty of blackmailing his own daughter, looking at it from a different perspective, Shane could understand a bit better how Edward wanted what he thought was best for his daughter.

"So, like you're not going to have the sheriff throw me out of town, are you?"

He raised his brow and looked at Sarah.

"I mentioned that Spencer was a good friend of yours. I was afraid that you'd send him after us."

Shane shook his head. "In fact, I'll buy your lunch." He looked directly at Mondo and added, "You can stay at the house while I get to know you."

"So you can talk us out of getting married?" Sarah asked suspiciously.

"I'd prefer you waited until after graduation."

He recognized the set of her chin. "And what if we still want to get married, anyway?"

He leveled his gaze at the couple. "I won't lose my sister."

"Would we get to share the bedroom?" Sarah asked, looking at her soda, not her brother.

He drummed his fingers. "You're not married yet."

"Just checking."

Shane paid the bill, then said, "I'll see you at home."

Sarah scrambled from the booth and hugged him tightly, stunning him.

"You're all I have in the world," she said. "I never knew Mom, then after Dad died, I thought I would, too. He wasn't a great father. He was drunk more times than he wasn't, but he was my dad. But you were always there for me, Shane. I'd die if I lost you."

He stroked her hair, hugging her back, realizing he hadn't done this for years. Maybe Angie was right; maybe he'd been more afraid of being hurt than of living.

"We'll wait to get married, Shane."

"Thank you," he said with a relieved sigh.

"You're my hero. Did I ever tell you that?"

He ruffled her hair, grinning.

Mondo stood and offered his hand. "Thanks for being so cool to Sarah."

"I could say the same to you."

"Cool, man."

"We'll be home later. I want to introduce Mondo to a few friends."

He nodded, his gut no longer in a knot.

"Hey, Shane?"

"Yeah?"

"Don't let Angie get away again."

Shaking his head, he left.

Hardhat yawned, then clambered back up front to sit in the passenger seat.

This time, when Shane reached the tree where he'd proposed to Angie, he stopped, too.

Saving his relationship with Sarah meant the world to him. And he had Angie to thank. He doubted pride would have let him go after her. She'd have left him, as surely as Angie had.

He turned on the radio and cranked up the volume as he drove home, hoping music would drown his thoughts.

It didn't.

The Shania Twain song that Angie had been singing and dancing to made the speakers vibrate. He listened to the words, and realized he wasn't the kind of man she needed, never would be. Giving orders came easily to him, protecting others was second nature. And she'd had enough of both.

Hardhat ran through the snow when they arrived at the cabin, his back legs skidding out from beneath him. Indignantly he picked himself up, shook his head, then took off after a squirrel.

Shane's house was cold, empty and lonely.

There were no soft sighs filling the room, but the traces of her still lingered.

The thought that he'd never have the opportunity to be with Angie again made his gut twist. Except for their work together, he'd never be alone with her. He wouldn't hear her secrets, share her excitement, be part of making a dream come true for the town. Suddenly his life felt very empty... Very lonely.

Weak winter sunlight splashed through the window and spilled a beam across the floor. He saw something gold glinting and he was drawn toward the closet.

Crouching, he saw Angie's golden aspen leaf lying on the carpet near the box where he'd kept her things. Without meaning to, he picked up the trinket, remembering the night he'd given it to her. He hadn't had lots of money back then, but Angie had acted as if he'd bought her the moon. As he'd fastened the necklace on her, she'd promised never to take it off.

His memory flashed to the night he'd come home and found her awful letter. Anger and hurt had surged in him as her betrayal seared him.

But as the gold, seemingly warm from the sun, lay in his palm, anger no longer consumed him.

He thought of her desertion, but differently. He recalled what she said about his argument with Sarah, the untenable situation he himself had put Sarah in.

With his thumb, he stroked the leaf's raised veins and, for the first time, saw the past from Angie's perspective.

Her father had had his fair share of faults, no doubt. But Angie had loved him, just as Sarah loved Shane. And Angie was right; if she'd told him about the ultimatum, he would have responded just the way she said.

He thought of Angie, young and vulnerable, faced with the impossible decision of whether to leave him or let her father destroy him and Sarah.

She'd done the only thing her heart would allow: break her own to save him. It was an unselfish act, one he suddenly realized he didn't deserve or appreciate.

He looked at the worn, dulled plating in his hand one more time.

He remembered his shock at seeing it around her neck after she battled her way through the storm to him. Her eyes had reflected love and adoration and her body had conformed oh-so-sweetly to his.

She'd never taken off the necklace, she'd said, at least not until he'd raged at her. She might have left him physically, but in her heart, she hadn't left him until he'd been an idiot.

At least that was something he had plenty of practice at, he thought bitterly.

He closed his hand around the inexpensive symbol of love, the love he'd callously thrown away, a love he wanted more than anything else.

Angie was quite a woman, full of love, energy and caring.... Rarely thinking of herself, she gave completely to others. Even now, when Shane had shut her out, she'd tried to save his relationship with his sister. Always, she thought of others first.

What a gift she'd offered, and how stupid of him to toss it in her face. If he hadn't been so focused on himself, maybe he would have seen that earlier....

He uncurled his hand again and stared at the one lasting memento of their love.

Was it too late? he wondered. Was it too late to tell her he cared, that he'd been wrong, that being alone was worse than being hurt, that he'd do anything for a second chance?

He'd never been good at swallowing his pride and letting anyone get close, but thanks to Angie, he'd tried with Sarah, and it had worked.

His heart added a few extra thumps as he pulled his wallet from his back pocket and slipped the necklace inside. On impulse, he gently lifted her engagement ring from the box and polished the diamond on the sleeve of his cotton shirt, praying he'd have the chance to slip it on her finger.

If he was going to win her love, he had to risk everything.

Hardhat barked and jumped in the four-wheel-drive vehicle as soon as Shane opened the door. "I don't know that we stand a chance, boy," Shane said, slipping the transmission into first gear.

His knuckles were white on the steering wheel as he drove through town, and he left the radio turned off. Hardhat cocked his head to one side, but he didn't make a sound.

Nerves ate at Shane as he drove to the Hot Springs Resort. Gwen greeted him warmly, then her smile faded when Shane asked what room Angie was in.

"Your Angie?"

His Angie. He liked the sound of that. "Yes."

"I'm sorry, Shane. I can't help you."

His mouth dry, he asked, "Can you at least call her room and ask if she'll see me?"

Gwen shook her head. "She was never here."

His heart sank. No. It wasn't possible. "She didn't check in?" Even to his own ears, the words sounded hollow.

She wouldn't take the chance of going back to the house; he knew that.

Which meant one thing: she'd left him.

Twelve

Shane refused to give up.

He hadn't come to his senses only to lose her.

Pushing the speed limit, he drove through town, checking the parking lots of the town's few hotels, looking at all the cars parked along Front Street, making sure she wasn't at the schoolhouse, then, his gut churning, he went to her aunt's house.

Her car was there.

He swore beneath his breath, both with relief that he'd found her and irritation that she was in a dangerous place when all he wanted to do was keep her safe.

Shutting off the engine, he started toward the house, taking the porch steps in a single stride. Hardhat on his heels, Shane rang the bell.

She didn't answer.

He rang again, longer and harder. Hardhat joined in with loud barks.

Shane heard sound coming from inside, but she still didn't respond. "Damn it," he called out, pounding forcefully on the door. "Open up, Angie."

The bolt slid open with a thump.

He dragged in a deep breath when he saw her.

"Did you find Sarah?"

He didn't want to talk about Sarah; he wanted to tell Angie what she meant to him. But he'd fallen in love with her for so many reasons, especially because of the way she cared about others. "Yes."

"So you went to town?"

"And I met Mondo."

She smoothed the front of her jeans with her hands.

"I won't lose my sister. Thank you for that."

Angie blinked and looked at him. "You're welcome. Is that all?"

Not by a long shot.

She started to close the door, and he put his foot inside the house. "Can I come in?"

She didn't budge. "I was just leaving."

"Going to the Hot Springs?" he asked, clearing his throat.

"Going to the Denver airport."

Hardhat wormed his way between them. After Angie petted him, he pushed the door open and darted inside.

Shane saw her suitcases near the stairs, packed and zipped, an airplane ticket on top.

"I changed my reservation. I have a flight tonight."

Damn it, he was out of time. And he wasn't at his best when it came to emotional issues. Fear of losing her shut all other thoughts out of his mind. He dragged his hand through his hair, then grabbed her shoulders. "Don't go," he implored.

She blinked, then looked up at him. "I beg your pardon?"

"I'm an idiot, a fool. You were right about everything, and I don't want to lose you."

"You already have," she said, her voice hoarse. "You sent me away."

Was she fighting tears? he wondered. And did that mean he still had a chance? "I love you, Angie. I always have. I always will. I loved the woman you were, and I adore the independent woman you are."

"You love..." Her mouth fell open in shock and he kissed her deeply, moving them both into the foyer and kicking the door closed.

When he slowly ended the kiss, he held on to her, mostly because he was scared beyond words that she'd get away. "You were right," he confessed. "About me, about everything. And I know my heart will break if you won't let me love you, but you're worth the gamble."

"I can't know that, Shane." Tears shimmered on her eyelashes and made her voice waver. "And I can't give up being who I am."

"I don't want you to." He squeezed tightly, desperate for her to understand. "There's a big difference between my kind of caring and the control Jack tried to exert over you. He was punishing you. I just want to care for you."

"Shane—"

"Does your organization have to be run from Chicago?"

"No, but—"

"But?"

"I'd have to travel frequently."

"Done."

"I'd need an office."

"I know someone in construction."

"I'd have to relocate my assistant."

"No problem."

She closed her eyes, shuttering the emotion. Her lower lip trembled and she shivered. "This isn't a negotiation," she said, finally looking at him.

"No. It's about making you happy, about me proving that I'm not Jack, that I've changed." Rolling the dice, he let go of her long enough to pull out his wallet and remove the aspen leaf. He draped the necklace over his forefinger. "Tell me about this."

She looked at the pendant for a moment, mesmerized.

"For five years you never took it off."

"No."

His heart hammered. "Why not?"

"Because it was a reminder I was loved," she whispered, looking at him through wide, luminescent blue eyes. Then, honesty in the set of her shoulders, she said, "It was also a reminder that I'd loved, too."

"And now?"

"Shane—"

"I love you, Angie." He closed one hand around the aspen leaf and slipped the other around the back of her neck, cradling her head. "Tell me you love me."

"I never stopped," she admitted. "But love's not enough." She tried to blink away the tears, but one fell, streaking onto her cheek. "I walked out once," she reminded him. "You don't trust me." Angie's voice broke, along with her heart. "I can't live like that, Shane."

Shane was offering the things she'd so desperately wanted to hear. Part of her wanted to throw herself forward, be captured in his strong arms and give herself over to a possibility. But cold reality had taught her that he didn't trust her.

"I believe in you, Angie."

She felt his hand on the back of her neck, demanding and reassuring at the same time. He unclenched his hand and her pendant lay there. The color was dulled, but the first rush of their love was still there, emphasized by the fact the gold no longer had the patina of newness. The very fact it was well-worn proved their commitment.

"As long as you're wearing this, how could I ever doubt you? As for me, I learned an important lesson today. You helped me see that the past was repeating itself."

He drew a shaky breath, and in his trembling shoulders, she saw how much the raw honesty cost him.

"I see why you sacrificed yourself for me and Sarah."

Somewhere deep inside, something—maybe her womb—tightened. "You can honestly see that?"

"Yeah. When I was at the diner with Sarah and Mondo..."

She smiled a little at the emphasis on the young man's name.

"I saw that she was stuck in the middle of two men, like you had been. Only I didn't have the leverage your father had. If it hadn't been for your father, you might never have left me."

"*Wouldn't* have left you," she corrected him.

He tightened his hold slightly. "Wouldn't have left me," he agreed. "Today I saw you fight for my sister. How could I believe you wouldn't fight for us?"

"Oh, Shane." He absently rubbed her nape and she felt her resistance ebbing. His vibrant green eyes were verdant with emotion.

"I almost lost Sarah. I don't want to lose you again

through my own stupidity. I went to the Hot Springs and learned you hadn't checked in. I drove around town like a crazy man looking for you. And right now I'm so damn scared, my knees are locked so I can stand up straight.''

This was more than she dared hope. Through her tears, she smiled.

''Take a chance on me, Angie. Say you'll marry me.''

He held up the aspen leaf and it glinted in the incandescent lighting. Wordlessly she turned her back to him and lifted her hair.

He kissed her there, sending a shock wave of pleasure all the way to her toes. After he fastened the clasp, he turned her to face him. He was grinning like a fool when he said, ''I'll love you forever.''

''And I'll love you a day longer than that,'' she swore.

He took out her ring and slid it onto her finger, then claimed her lips and her commitment, as she demanded his in return. Shane willingly gave it....

Epilogue

"**A**round the Town"
by Miss Starr
Excitement is in the air! Not only has Angela
Burton Masters remarried our own Shane, but
they've recently returned from a successful trip to
Chicago where she and her doting husband had a
fabulous Valentine's Day fund-raising gala for
Dreams and Wishes. And now it's our turn!

Angela and Shane will join forces the first
weekend of May to celebrate the grand opening
of the town's incredible community center. Rumor has it the opening will be an extravaganza
like this town has never seen. As well it should
be!

Miss Starr sneaked a peek (it is her duty to you,

my reader, after all) at the remodeled school-house, and I can say with certainty that Angela's vision has combined incredibly well with Shane's talents. The project was finished ahead of time and under budget. The children will enjoy this center for generations to come, thanks to Shane and Angela Masters.

Rumor has it that Angela will be wearing a dress she purchased during her Chicago trip, a gown her newly re-wed husband chose. It's black silk, and evidently the back is cut down to *there*. You'll recognize me tonight, gentle readers, I'll be the one blushing!

Since the whole town is invited, I'll see you there.

Until next week, this is all the news you can use.

"You look beautiful. Do you know that?"

Angie felt Shane's hand on her bare back and she jumped at the warm touch. He came up behind her and nuzzled her neck. "This grand re-opening is a huge success, thanks to you, Mrs. Masters."

She turned into her husband's arms and placed her fingertip in that tempting cleft in his chin. "Thanks to your awesome talents, Mr. Masters. We make a good team."

"A hell of a team," he agreed.

He smelled masculine, of the mountain outdoors and spice. He'd made love to her before they'd left for the night, and suddenly she wanted him again.

"I knew this dress was hot, but I didn't know it'd make me want to take your clothes off in public."

She grinned and ran her fingers across his satiny bow tie.

Just as he was going to kiss her, Nick Andrews slapped him on the back. "Great job, Masters."

Shane grimaced and she nearly laughed. He mouthed "later" to her, and a shiver traced down her exposed spine.

He turned to face his friend, but reached protectively for Angie's elbow and cupped it with his palm.

"Noelle will get a chance to use the center," Lilly said, coming over and gently pinching Nick's arm for interrupting Shane and Angie. "Thanks for building it."

Angie's heart soared. She loved making a difference, and with Shane at her side, it was even more thrilling. True to his word, he supported her in every way, and the love she came home to filled her heart. She accomplished more than she ever had, finding that a happy marriage gave her twice as much stamina. Not only that, but Shane was so full of ideas himself, the partnership was incredible. "Where is the little one?"

"With Bernadette," Lilly said. "I think I'm ready to have my daughter back."

"It's been two minutes," Nick said.

"You're just as bad as me," Lilly protested. Then she said to Angie and Shane, "We went to the movies the other night and left Noelle with Kurt and Jessie. It was our first date since Noelle was born. Nick couldn't stand being away from his little girl, so we left during the opening credits."

Shane raised his brow, and Nick said, "Guilty."

Kurt and Jessie joined them, and Jessie definitely

glowed. Kurt kept glancing at his wife solicitously and even once whispered in her ear, asking if she needed anything.

Bernadette Simpson joined the party with a fussy Noelle.

Nick took his daughter and placed her against his tuxedoed shoulder.

She quieted instantly and Jessie asked Kurt, "Are you taking notes?"

"I'm ready."

They shared a private glance and Angie couldn't resist looking at Shane. Just last night, they'd talked about starting a family of their own....

Bernadette "ahemed" and asked, "Now that you're married, who's next?"

Slade Birmingham walked in, Stetson tipped rakishly, boots gleaming in a way that matched the sudden twinkle in Bernadette's eye. "If you'll excuse me," she said. "I wonder how things are going with setting up the computer system at his ranch? And isn't Rachel Kincade trying to start a computer business?"

She sashayed off, her long silk dress whispering.

Lilly frowned. "Do you suppose she's..."

"Miss Starr?" Angie asked.

"No," Kurt said. "I thought it was Bridget from the Chuckwagon."

"Or Gwen from the Hot Springs Resort."

Still, Angie wondered...

"We're here!"

Sarah burst through the door, all energy and exuberance, Mondo holding her hand. Mondo looked respectable, Angie thought with a grin, if you didn't count the fact he hadn't tucked in his tuxedo shirt. Unfortunately, the label was exposed, but Sarah didn't seem to mind. Her hand was enfolded in the crook of his arm and she positively beamed.

"The party can begin!" Sarah said.

Shane shook Mondo's hand and hugged Sarah. Angie smiled. She'd gotten a wonderful husband, lots of support and a younger sister whom she adored. Sarah had even been Angie's maid of honor. Her recent fund-raiser had earned more than she dared dream, and she was surrounded by family, trust and love. Shane was only demanding out of concern, and she decided she could live with that. Life didn't get any better.

Shane was thinking much the same thing.

Later, when everyone had gone, he tipped his champagne glass to her. "You were incredible. Congratulations."

"Couldn't have done it without you."

Even though there was no music and the cleanup crew was working, he put down their glasses and guided her to the dance floor...any excuse to have her in his loving arms.

He never thought he'd open his heart, let alone love again. But Angie had been worth the risk. Even though she had on an expensive dress, she still wore the aspen leaf, the pendant nestled between her breasts. She loved him, and he marveled at that. She was the woman who was meant to be his mate and he told her so.

She shuddered and leaned into him, so reminiscent of the way she'd flung herself into his arms during the blizzard a few months ago. They became motionless on the floor and she silently sealed his words with a kiss.

He was suddenly grateful for the blizzard and the one snowbound weekend she thought she was his wife.

She'd made his dreams come true. "I'll spend a lifetime making your dreams come true," he said. Then he swung her into his arms and carried her to the car, intent on taking her home and proving it to her, again and again....

*   *   *   *   *

FORTUNE'S Children™

*The Fortune family requests
your presence at the weddings of*

*Silhouette Desire's provocative new miniseries
featuring the beloved Fortune family and
five of your favorite authors.*

Bride of Fortune—August 2000
by Leanne Banks (SD #1311)

Mail-Order Cinderella—September 2000
by Kathryn Jensen (SD #1318)

Fortune's Secret Child—October 2000
by Shawna Delacorte (SD #1324)

Husband—or Enemy?—November 2000
by Caroline Cross (SD #1330)

Groom of Fortune—December 2000
by Peggy Moreland (SD #1336)

*Don't miss these unforgettable romances...
available at your favorite retail outlet.*

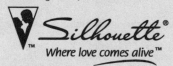

Where love comes alive™

**Don't miss
an exciting opportunity
to save on the purchase of
Harlequin and Silhouette books!**

Buy any two Harlequin or
Silhouette books and save
$10.00 off future Harlequin
and Silhouette purchases

OR

buy any three
Harlequin or Silhouette books
and save **$20.00 off** future
Harlequin and Silhouette purchases.

**Watch for details
coming in October 2000!**

PHQ400

COMING NEXT MONTH

#1315 SLOW WALTZ ACROSS TEXAS—Peggy Moreland
Man of the Month/Texas Grooms

Growing up an orphan had convinced cowboy Clayton Rankin that he didn't need anyone. But when his wife, Rena, told him he was about to lose her, he was determined to win back her love—and have his wife teach him about matters of the heart!

#1316 ROCK SOLID—Jennifer Greene
Body & Soul

She needed to unwind. But when Lexie Woolf saw Cash McKay, relaxation was the last thing on her mind. Cash was everything Lexie had dreamed of in a man—except she feared *she* was not the woman for *him*. Could Cash convince Lexie that their love was rock solid?

#1317 THE NEXT SANTINI BRIDE—Maureen Child
Bachelor Battalion

They were supposed to be together for only one night of passion, but First Sergeant Dan Mahoney couldn't forget Angela Santini. So he set out to seduce the single mom—one tantalizing touch at a time—and convince her that all her nights were meant to be spent with him!

#1318 MAIL-ORDER CINDERELLA—Kathryn Jensen
Fortune's Children: The Grooms

Tyler Fortune needed a bride—and plain librarian Julie Parker fit the bill. But Tyler never counted on falling for his convenient wife. Now he needed to convince Julie that she was the perfect mate for him—so he could become her husband in every way.

#1319 LADY WITH A PAST—Ryanne Corey

She thought no one knew of her former notoriety, but when Connor Garrett tracked down Maxie Calhoon, she had to face her past. Connor stirred emotions in Maxie that she had never experienced, but did he love the woman she once was or the one she had become?

#1320 DOCTOR FOR KEEPS—Kristi Gold

The last thing Dr. Rick Jansen needed was to fall for his new nurse, Miranda Brooks. Yet there was something about Miranda that made it impossible to keep his thoughts—and hands—away from her. But would he still desire Miranda when he learned her secret?